"She's a leech," said a now-familiar voice from across the room.

Nell turned and stared at the man who'd rescued her from the roadside. The billowing black coat was gone and now she saw a solidly built man, holding a steaming mug, in dark jeans and a black knit sweater stalk across the room. He bent low to drop a kiss upon the older woman's downy wrinkled cheek, then stood in front of the fire, all tall and brooding, as he warmed his hands.

"A leech?" asked his granny.

"He means I'm a phlebotomist. I take people's blood," she clarified.

"And goes out and drives in dangerous weather for no reason," he mumbled as he sipped at his drink.

She glared at him. "I was not out for no reason! You know, you're very rude. I just hope your bedside manner makes you a much better doctor than you are a human being."

He took another sip from his coffee, contemplating a sharp retort, but thought better of it. Because each time she argued with him, he felt a stirring within his blood that he didn't want to think too hard about.

Dear Reader,

Sometimes you get the urge to write a Christmas story, and I knew I had to write one when I got the image in my head of a stubborn grieving mother stuck in a ditch during a blizzard. I knew her name was Nell and I truly felt like I knew who she was. Why she was there. Why she was out in such weather, when everyone else was wise enough to stay at home and not risk the roads. And once I had Nell, I had to give her a strong hero to counterbalance her.

And along came Seth.

I wish I could show you my vision board for Seth! He was a whole mood! And once I'd fallen in love with him, I knew—hoped—you readers would too. Nell and Seth get off to an antagonistic start, but sometimes they're the most fun to write, and when they move past that stage and their relationship becomes something deeper? It becomes something magical.

So, I hope you'll enjoy my little Christmas story.

Nell and Seth are waiting for you, just as they were waiting for each other.

Happy reading!

Louisa x

SNOWED IN WITH THE CHILDREN'S DOCTOR

LOUISA HEATON

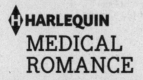

HARLEQUIN

MEDICAL
ROMANCE

HARLEQUIN®
MEDICAL ROMANCE™

Recycling programs
for this product may
not exist in your area.

ISBN-13: 978-1-335-59503-4

Snowed In with the Children's Doctor

Copyright © 2023 by Louisa Heaton

For questions and comments about the quality of this book, please contact us at CustomerService@Harlequin.com.

Harlequin Enterprises ULC
22 Adelaide St. West, 41st Floor
Toronto, Ontario M5H 4E3, Canada
www.Harlequin.com

Printed in U.S.A.

Louisa Heaton lives on Hayling Island, Hampshire, with her husband, four children and a small zoo. She has worked in various roles in the health industry—most recently four years as a community first responder, answering 999 calls. When not writing, Louisa enjoys other creative pursuits, including reading, quilting and patchwork—usually instead of the things she *ought* to be doing!

Books by Louisa Heaton

Harlequin Medical Romance

Greenbeck Village GPs

The Brooding Doc and the Single Mom
Second Chance for the Village Nurse

Reunited at St. Barnabas's Hospital

Twins for the Neurosurgeon

The Prince's Cinderella Doc
Pregnant by the Single Dad Doc
Healed by His Secret Baby
The Icelandic Doc's Baby Surprise
Risking Her Heart on the Trauma Doc
A Baby to Rescue Their Hearts
A GP Worth Staying For
Their Marriage Meant To Be
Their Marriage Worth Fighting For
A Date with Her Best Friend
Miracle Twins for the Midwife

Visit the Author Profile page at Harlequin.com.

For Soraya, my editor, who helped me tremendously to whip this story into shape!

**Praise for
Louisa Heaton**

"Ms. Heaton pens a story that is sure to keep the reader engaged and cheering her characters on in their journey to a HEA and this one is up there with the best…. This really is a beautiful moving story…I do highly recommend for anyone who loves a good romance."
—*Goodreads* on *Pregnant by the Single Dad Doc*

CHAPTER ONE

'YES, THANK YOU very much, Joe. Well, for anyone who's got a window, it is snowing heavily
here in the Midlands. A large area of low pressure has been moving up the country, bringing
with it *unprecedented* amounts of snow, and it
looks like we'll have this for at least the next
twenty-four hours. Experts are predicting *over
ten inches* of snow to fall over the next few
hours, causing drifts, whiteouts and generally
hazardous conditions. People are being advised
not to travel, unless *absolutely* essential, and
if you do, please take precautions. Visibility is
down to just a few metres in some more rural
areas, so do take care. Here at Clifton FM,
we'll be bringing you all the latest weather re-
ports on the hour, every hour...'

There was a burst of Christmas pop music,
with jingle bells.

Nell reached forward to turn down the car
radio. It was just what she'd expected to hear

from the traffic report. The weathermen on television, before she'd set out, had advised against travel, too. But nothing—no snow, no blizzard, no unprecedented area of low pressure—was *ever* going to stop her from visiting Lucas's grave on the anniversary of his death.

It was just snow, after all. There'd never been this amount of panic over a bit of snow when she'd been a child. Not like today. It was health and safety gone mad.

So it was dark. Evening. Yes, the snow was heavy, and the wiper blades on her car were having trouble clearing the thick white flakes that blew against her windscreen. And, yes, she was creeping along in low gear, because drifts were already forming, sweeping up to meet hedgerows and tree trunks. And, yes, visibility was bad, and this part of the road didn't have streetlamps, but it was perfectly doable. All she had to do was stay on the road.

Which, she had to admit, was difficult, because she was on a remote country lane, near Elmbridge Manor and this was a notorious spot even on clear days. She'd lost count of how many times she'd read about an accident here when visibility was bad. Deep ditches on either side of the road, lots of bends and curves, like a sinuous snake… Normally the lane was edged with dark, spiny hedgerows, but tonight even those were covered in snow. Everything looked white.

It was difficult to judge, but she figured if she just stayed in the centre then everything would be—

A deer suddenly leapt over her car, hooves clipping the bonnet, and Nell screamed and yanked the wheel in panic, sending the car spinning on the ice beneath the snow and plummeting into the left-hand ditch with a sudden, sickening thud.

She found herself gasping, heart pounding, her entire world tilted by forty-five degrees, the back end of her car sticking up, her mad wipers going as fast as her heart.

'Oh, my God! Oh, my God...' Her whole body trembling, she burst into tears.

This was not how today was meant to end! She'd wanted to do what she always did. Lay flowers on Lucas's grave, then drive home and watch his favourite Christmas movie whilst wrapped up in a blanket, sobbing quietly to herself whilst she ate giant amounts of Lucas's favourite ice cream. Mint choc chip.

It was something she'd done the first year after losing him, on the anniversary of his death. Without thinking. Doing the things that he'd enjoyed in a bid to feel closer to him. To pretend that he was near. And now it had just become a thing. She'd done it last year, too, and today she'd known for sure what she was going to do because she recognised it as a routine. A self-soothing ritual that marked the day of his passing.

She'd made it to the cemetery. Laid a wreath at his grave, staring at his name etched into the stone as the thick flakes had swarmed around her in the strong winds. How long she'd stood there she didn't know. Only when the cold had begun to penetrate her bones, and her toes and fingers had gone completely numb, had she walked back to her car and begun the drive home.

And now she and the car were stuck in a muddy, icy ditch in the middle of nowhere, miles away from home and with no idea how she'd get there.

Nell searched blindly for her phone, but it had fallen from its place in the middle of the console and into the passenger footwell. She unclipped her seatbelt and leant forward to reach for it, cursing and swearing quietly until her fingers grasped its leather cover and she pulled it to her, looking for the small card that held the details of her breakdown cover.

She'd never called them before, but she'd seen an advert on the television for them recently, telling their customers that they'd be treated like family and that if you were a woman, stranded alone, then you'd be made a priority customer. She hoped that would be true as she dialled the number, listening to the robotic voice telling her all the options before she finally got through to a human being.

'Oh, thank God! Yes, I've had an accident and my car's in a ditch. A deer leapt across the road.'

Had it been a deer? She could have sworn it was a reindeer, complete with jingle bells, now that she thought about it, but that couldn't be right. She'd not been drinking, so why would she think it had jingle bells?

'I'm by myself…can you get someone out to me?'

She'd already tapped in her membership number, but the young man called Evan, on the other end, apologised. He told her that because of the extreme weather they didn't have anyone free to help her right now, but someone should be with her within a few hours.

'A few hours? What am I supposed to do whilst I wait? Freeze to death?'

'I'm so sorry, Miss Bryant, but we simply don't have enough technicians free. As I'm sure you can appreciate, with this freak weather we're having, the demands on our services are unprecedented.'

Unprecedented. There was that damn word again. She'd got sick of hearing it during the Covid pandemic and now it seemed people used it all the time.

'Do you have anything in the vehicle to keep you warm?'

She had a blanket. But with the engine off and all that snow outside how warm would she be?

'Maybe...'

'Are there any properties nearby that you could go to? Knock at the door and see if they could help?'

She shook her head. 'No. This area's remote.'

She knew she was on a lane at the rear of the Elmbridge Manor estate, but there were a few acres between her and the house and she couldn't imagine tramping through all that snow just to speak to some snobby butler, or something. And there were obviously wild deer around here! Also, if she remembered correctly, a lake in the grounds somewhere.

What if she were to fall in? Because the snow would have covered that, too, over the ice that must have frozen it over in the preceding weeks.

'Well, then we advise you stay with your vehicle, Miss Bryant, until help arrives.'

Nell ended the call, feeling so angry she wanted to throw the phone back into the passenger footwell. But she didn't want to break it. She might need it again.

The breakdown service had been useless! But, to be fair, it was probably to be expected. She had been warned against coming out in this blizzard and yet she had stubbornly refused to let a bit of bad weather stop her. It was hugely important to her that she visited Lucas on important days. His birthday. Easter—which he'd loved. Halloween. Christmas. The anniversary of the day that he'd passed.

She couldn't look after him any more, but she could look after his gravesite. Keep it neat. Tidy. Weed-free. With fresh flowers whenever she could. He wasn't here any more, but she felt close to him there. Felt that she could talk to him still. It gave her comfort. She was still of a mind that her journey had been essential. A mother needing to be with her son. What could be more important than that?

But now…? She sat in the dark car as it filled with shadow, the snow blocking out the available moonlight. How long she sat there she didn't know. Thirty minutes? Forty?

She glanced at her phone.

Just over an hour!

The chill had penetrated the car and outside looked just as bad as ever. Should she get out and walk? Try and stick to the road? If she walked in the direction she'd been headed, she'd come to a house in about two miles…

She vaguely became aware that the inside of her car had brightened slightly, as if another car was approaching from behind. Nell turned to peer through the rear windshield, but the snow was thick upon the glass, allowing only glimmers of light through the flakes and frozen crystals. Could she hear an engine?

The light stilled and she heard the noise of a car door slamming and then the heavy thud of footsteps. It looked as if whoever it was had a torch. Light flashed this way, then that. She heard a curse. Maybe someone stumbling.

Should she lock her doors? It could be anyone. Her fear manifested itself first. This was such a remote road and she hadn't seen any other cars for ages. It would be the perfect spot to take advantage of a woman on her own. But her fear was balanced equally with the desire to get home as quickly as possible. And if she was inclined to believe that someone was coming to attack her, surely she ought also to believe that this could be her knight in shining armour.

Or dame in shining armour…

Her heart hammered in her chest as the person outside got closer and a darker shadow passed over her car door. Whoever it was looked tall. Powerful.

A sudden rap on the window made her jump.

Of all the stupid things in all the world to be doing in weather like this, Dr Seth James, Lord Elmbridge, had not expected to be out rounding up escaped reindeer. On nights like these, when the windchill factor had dropped the temperature considerably, and every gust felt as if the world was trying to take a bite out of his face, he'd have much preferred to be indoors, before a roaring fire in the drawing room of his private quarters, enjoying a nice glass of his finest whisky.

But, no. The heavy snowfall had spelled the death of the fencing at the reindeer enclosure. Its posts had given up the ghost and begun to lean heavily, and before he'd known it, he'd had a call from Ned Hoskins, who lived at Hilltop Farm, to say that he'd got reindeer wandering about his cowsheds and did he want to fetch them before they made it to the village?

The reindeer had been Granny's idea. She'd thought it would be a fine final touch to the Christmas Experience they offered at Elmbridge Manor. They had Santa, and a grotto, and even some well-paid elves to help corral the children who would wait in line with their parents to meet St Nicholas and his endless sack of free gifts, and she'd suggested that this year they have reindeer too. Decked out with jingle bells. The whole shebang.

And he'd agreed. Stupidly. Not realising how much extra work the reindeer would be. But then again, why would he? He was a paediatrician, not a reindeer farmer, and when he'd hired the reindeer for the festive season he'd thought he'd also hired an experienced reindeer wrangler. Only Sven had finished early for the day, when the snow had begun to fall thick and heavy, citing that he wanted to be back home with his heavily pregnant girlfriend, just in case she went into labour.

Fair enough. Seth remembered the anxiety he'd felt himself as Dana's due date had got closer and closer, and they'd not even had to worry about snow. Dana had been pregnant through summer, complaining only about the heat.

And so, instead of warming himself before that roaring fireplace, he'd instead donned his thickest coat, scarf, gloves and boots and headed out into the cold to hitch the trailer to the back of his car.

He had not been happy about it. Every newsreader, every weatherman, had warned people about going out in these conditions, but what else was he to do? Let the reindeer terrorise the local village? If they'd already made it to Hilltop, then they were only a mile or so away from people's homes, and he didn't want to imagine the calls the local police would get when the villagers started to notice giant deer in their back gardens.

And he didn't want the animals being darted by animal control and taken away—not when he'd paid for them and they were in his care.

It had been a difficult hour or two at Hilltop. Up there, exposed to the most biting winds of this blizzard, he and Ned, with the help of his sheepdogs, Buzz and Rex, had managed to round up eight of the nine reindeer into the back of his trailer, which he'd filled with warming hay and straw. One was still missing, and hadn't been found anywhere.

Ned had invited him in for a warming hot cocoa, but Seth had declined. He'd wanted to get back. Put the reindeer in the stables opposite the horses, so that tomorrow he could work on the fencing and get that sorted. He'd just have to hope the ninth reindeer showed up somewhere.

It had been a long day. He hadn't been able to feel his fingers. His toes. His nose had to be as red as Rudolph's...

And then, to top off the perfect evening, he'd been driving back to Elmbridge and had got to that sharp turning at the rear of the estate, the part of the road that had taken Dana's life, when he'd seen the fading taillights of a car in the left-hand ditch.

A sick feeling had made his stomach feel like lead. He'd stopped and sat there for a moment. Staring at the car that was already half covered by snow and in a drift, frozen in place. It had been as if he couldn't move. As if he'd been thrown back in time, pinned in place by fear and dread.

But then his medical instincts had kicked in. *Someone might need help.*

They were most likely okay…had just driven off the road, that was all.

Switching on his own hazard lights, he'd grabbed a torch from the glove box and got out into the blizzard, wincing at the icy touch of every snowflake blasting into his face. He'd felt the snow gathering on his face. On his beard. His eyebrows. His shoulders. Felt the cold sinking in through the thick woollen coat that was now splashed with mud.

He'd tramped through the snow, wondering who on earth had been stupid enough to come out in this weather when the whole world and his wife had been telling everyone to stay indoors except for emergencies.

When his boot had slipped on some hidden ice and he'd fallen to one knee, he'd cursed and sworn like a sailor, before getting to his feet once again and tramping angrily over to the car.

Now he rapped the torch against the driver's window.

At first he thought that the driver must have walked off to look for help, but then the car door cracked open an inch.

'Hello…?'

The thickness of the blizzard stopped him from seeing who was inside, but the voice sounded like a woman's.

'Are you all right? Can I help?'

Okay, so maybe he didn't sound as friendly as he'd wanted to. But he was exhausted, cold, muddy, and now his knee hurt from the slip on the ice. He just wanted to be at home with Granny and Olly. He didn't get to see much of his son, what with work, and now that he'd started his first year at school he'd been hoping to spend some quality time with him. Not be out at all hours rounding up reindeer and helping a woman out of a ditch.

The door closed slightly. 'Who are you?'

He still couldn't see her face in the darkness

and through the blizzard, but he really wanted this to be over sooner rather than later.

He shone the torch on his own face. 'I'm a doctor. I work at the local hospital.'

'I don't recognise you.'

Seth frowned. What the hell was that supposed to mean? 'It was my first day today and it's a big hospital. Who are you?'

Two could play at this game.

'I'm a phlebotomist.'

A vampire. One of those people you could call on to come and take blood and place IVs because doctors were too busy to do everything.

'What are you doing out in this storm? Don't you know it's dangerous?' he asked, just as the wind howled in response, whipping around him in a gust designed to lift him off his feet.

But Seth was tall and broad and, he thought, strong. It would take more than a blizzard to move him.

'You think I'm stupid? Of course I know.'

'Then why are you out?'

There was a brief pause, then the door was pushed open and a woman in a long puffer coat, beanie and thick scarf attempted to climb out of the car.

But her car was at an odd angle and it was not an elegant disembarkation.

Seth stifled a wry smile as he watched her awkwardly clamber out, cursing and muttering to herself as she tried to do so with dignity. He'd seen more graceful newborn giraffes. He proffered a hand, but she glaringly refused to take it.

'Do you not have roadside assistance?' he asked.

She turned to glare at him. 'They can't make it—they have no one free.'

'How long have you been here?'

'Long enough to think I'd be found years into the future trapped in the permafrost.'

'And you didn't go for help?'

She stared at him as if he was an idiot. 'From where, exactly? Are you familiar with this area?'

'A little.'

'Then you'd know there isn't anywhere to ask for help from around here—unless you fancy tramping a mile or so across unknown ground to beg for help from some crusty landowner.'

Crusty landowner? Hmm...

'So you thought you'd take a drive in the worst weather this area has experienced in a decade. Pray tell me what was so important you had to come out in this?'

'*You're* out. Why are *you* out?'

She peered past him to his four-by-four and trailer. But he could hardly tell her he was out rounding up lost reindeer. It sounded crazy even to him.

'Rescue mission. You?'

She didn't meet his gaze. She looked uncomfortable. 'Well, as much as I'm enjoying this inquisition at the roadside, I'm wondering if you can you help me or not?'

He could. 'I've got ropes.'

She nodded. 'Wonderful.'

'We can attach them to the rear of your vehicle and pull you out.'

'If it's not too much trouble.'

It was. He'd wanted to be warm and back home with his son by now. He gave a mock bow. 'You're welcome.'

She didn't seem thankful. Not really. She seemed pissed off—which was fine, because so was he. He still had no idea what she was doing out on a night like this. Clearly it wasn't a good reason or she would have told him. Instead, she'd evaded the question, which made him think that she'd thought that her errand—most likely something trivial or stupid—was too important to put off. She'd probably popped out to get a pint of milk.

Muttering under his breath, he fetched the ropes and began to attach them to both vehicles. He was aware of her standing back and watching him, hands crossed over her chest, rubbing at each arm as she jiggled to keep warm in one spot. It was hard to tie the knots with no feeling in his fingers, but somehow he managed it, and then he told her to stand back whilst he got back into his own vehicle and began to reverse, hoping to pull her car from the ditch.

It was a struggle. The snow had grown thick and deep around her car, and because of the width of the lane and the fact that he had the trailer behind his own vehicle, he couldn't get the angle he needed to pull the car out. It just kept sliding back through the ditch.

It was pointless.

After much toing and froing, he let out a heavy sigh and got out of his vehicle. 'It's no use. I can't get it free.'

She looked at him, frowning above her thick knitted scarf, already rimmed with snow. 'What am I going to do?'

'Anyone you can call to pick you up?'

'No.'

Damn. He couldn't leave her out here, stranded. 'I can drive you back to my home. You can stay warm, let people know you're all right. Sort something out...' He shrugged.

She peered at him. 'You could be anyone. An axe murderer.'

He showed her his empty hands. 'No axe.'

'A normal murderer, then.'

Really? He didn't have to put up with this crap. He was cold! He wanted a warm bath. Not to be dealing with this prickly phlebotomist.

'Fine. I'll see you around.' He began to tramp back towards his car.

'Wait! Are you just going to leave me here?'

He turned. 'I offered you a lift. Shelter. If I recall, you're the one who'd rather stay here. And, as warm as your manner is, it's not enough to make me want to stay with you.' He got into his vehicle, slammed the door.

She came over to his window and knocked on it.

He pressed the button to lower it. 'Yes?'

She looked torn. 'Well…where do you live? Close by?'

He nodded. 'Pretty close.'

'Where?'

'Elmbridge Manor.'

A frown and then a raising of her eyebrows. 'The Manor?'

He nodded again. Smiled. 'Crusty landowner—at your service.'

began to move away from her accident site she risked another glance at her dark-eyed saviour.

'Who were you rescuing?'

He frowned. 'What?'

'You said you were out on a rescue mission. Who were you rescuing? Or do you just drive around in snowstorms, looking for damsels in distress?'

'It's not a who—they're a what,' he answered grimly.

Nell frowned. 'What?'

'Reindeer. I was rescuing some reindeer that had escaped their enclosure.'

Reindeer? So maybe I wasn't hallucinating!

'Were they by any chance wearing jingle bells?'

He risked a glance at her. 'Why do you ask?'

'Because one of them leapt over my bloody car and caused the damned accident in the first place! I should sue you!'

'Sue *me*? What were you doing out and about in this weather? Did your nails need doing?'

His sarcastic tone did nothing to appease her. 'Don't be ridiculous!'

'Then why were you out?'

She clammed up. She did not have to explain herself to this man. Even if he was helping her.

They drove in silence for a while. The snow

was blowing onto the windscreen. And then he was indicating a right turn and pulling past two enormous gatehouses before heading up a long, partially cleared driveway to a house that she had only ever seen from the road.

Elmbridge Manor. A vast mansion of a house. Beautifully lit up with white fairy lights and multitudes of lit Christmas trees.

She wanted to gaze upon it and soak it all in, or even ask some questions, but she wouldn't give him the satisfaction. All she wanted was to get warm, call her breakdown service and let them know where she was, and how they could contact her when they finally arrived at the scene of her accident. Then she could go home and never see this man ever again! Because, like he said, it was a big hospital with hundreds of staff. They might never cross paths again.

He pulled up in front of the main doors. 'Ring the bell.'

'Don't you have a key?'

He smirked. 'I need to get the reindeer into their stables, which are at the rear of the property, so would you please ring the bell? Jeffreys will let you in.'

'Jeffreys?'

'The butler.'

'You have *a butler*?'

'Who else would open the door?'

A wry smile crept across her face. 'Right. Well, thank you, Mr Lord of the Manor, for your assistance. I will get out of your way as fast as I possibly can.'

'I will enjoy that very much, Miss I Should Never Have Been Out In This Weather.'

She got out and smirked at him before slamming the car door, hoping the vehemence of her slam would tell him just what she thought of him. As he drove away, she was very tempted to follow up with a hand gesture, but the wind was howling and she was getting cold again, so she did as he'd asked her and hurried to the doorway and rang the bell.

She thought for a moment that no one would answer, and that perhaps this was all an elaborate joke and maybe there were hidden cameras somewhere, when the door swung open and she saw a butler dressed in smart black and white peering at her in enquiry.

Jeffreys led her into a vast hall with a chequerboard floor and the tallest Christmas tree she had ever seen. Adorned with lights and baubles in tasteful rose golds and soft pinks, it looked like something she'd see in a huge American department store.

Beyond that were vast hanging tapestries

and two suits of armour guarding a sweeping staircase that wouldn't have looked out of place on the *Titanic*. Her gaze was drawn up along the fir-and-pinecone-laden balustrades, past a multitude of oil paintings of lords and ladies of old, to the vast arched dome of the ceiling, adorned with carvings and grotesques, a fresco of a hunting scene, and the biggest crystal chandelier she had ever seen in her entire life.

It was so big it would probably take up her entire bedroom, and it put the cheap, fringed flowery lampshade that she'd bought for her living room in a sale to shame.

'Wow.'

Briefly, she forgot how cold she was. How damp her clothes felt. Awe and wonder were the order of the day.

The grumpy doctor lived *here?*

She'd always been curious about this place, driving past it each day on her way to work. Elmbridge Manor was open to the public on most days of the year, and although she'd always told herself that one day she'd join a tour and take a look around, see how the other half lived, she had never quite organised the time. She'd been so busy with Lucas, and then he'd got sick, and then her marriage had broken down after he had died.

After that there just hadn't seemed any point. She'd thrown herself into her work, taken on extra shifts so she didn't have to stay at home alone, in her poky little flat. Listening to the silence. Living in that Lucas-free space. She already had so much missing from her life—she didn't want to see how rich other people's lives were compared to her own.

'May I take your coat, madam?' asked Jeffreys.

'Oh… Sure.'

Unused to such attention, Nell hadn't noticed the butler patiently waiting and watching her. She was going to just shrug it off, but then she paused as she saw Jeffreys was standing behind her to help her off with it. She blushed, embarrassed, and really not used to people serving her.

'Thank you. You're very kind.'

Jeffreys neatly folded her cheap puffer coat over his arm. 'Lord Elmbridge is unavailable at the moment, madam, but might I be allowed to show you into the drawing room?'

'Oh. Yes. Of course.'

Nell followed the silver-haired butler across the hall and through two large double doors into a room that was bigger than her entire flat. It was filled with baroque-inspired furniture, with walls lined in what appeared to be pale green silk, and her gaze was instantly drawn to the large fire crackling away beneath a huge stone mantelpiece.

'Would you like some refreshments, madam?'

'I wouldn't want to be any bother...'

'It's no bother, madam. Something warming, perhaps? Tea? Cocoa? Hot chocolate?'

Hot chocolate sounded amazing. She'd not had one since Lucas had been alive. 'Hot chocolate, please.'

Jeffreys gave a polite bow and disappeared from the room.

As she stood in front of the fire, hands out, enjoying the warm embrace of the flames, she let her gaze drift upwards to the portrait above the fireplace.

It was of an elderly gentleman, with white hair and thick white mutton chops either side of his frowning face. He wore wire-rimmed spectacles and at his feet lay two hunting dogs.

Peregrine Edward James, Fifth Lord Elmbridge, she mouthed, reading the inscription beneath.

'My husband,' said a woman's voice behind her.

Nell turned and smiled, blushing slightly. This woman probably had no idea who she was, or why she was standing in her drawing room. 'He looks a very fine gentleman.'

'He was a bloody awful man and I'm glad he's gone.'

Nell's mouth dropped open in amused shock.

'But portraits always make people look finer than they actually are.' The old woman smiled and hobbled towards her, using a cane. 'I'm Emily James. Dowager of this fine house. And you are…?' She peered up at her, with rheumy, kind eyes.

'Nell Bryant. I live in Clifton, but my car went into a ditch and a young man helped me out and brought me here.'

'Which young man?'

'Er…tall, dark hair. Bearded. Lives here?' she said, as if this might still be some joke and her rescuer was actually the groundskeeper, or something.

A warm smile crossed the Dowager's face. 'My grandson. Lovely boy. Heart of gold. Nothing like that one.' The Dowager indicated the painting again and then ambled over to one of the dark red sofas and slowly lowered herself onto it.

Nell stared at her in surprise, deciding she liked this older woman immensely.

'Do sit down, dear. You'll give me a crick in my neck.' The older woman pointed at the other sofa opposite her.

'I'm waiting for my breakdown people to arrive.'

'In this weather? You'll be lucky if you see them before morning.'

Nell's heart sank. Morning? The clock on the mantelpiece told her it was nearly eight o clock at night. She couldn't impose on these people for that long—it wouldn't be right.

'Maybe if I give them another ring...'

'Nonsense! Stay here tonight. There's no going anywhere—not in this storm.'

'I wouldn't want to impose.'

'You wouldn't be.'

'Well, only if you have the room. I'll sleep anywhere.'

'My dear, there are sixteen bedrooms in this place. We have more than enough room.'

She reached out and pulled a bellpull beside her chair. It must be connected to something in the staff quarters, because before she knew it, a maid had appeared in the doorway.

'Ava, my dear, would you prepare a guest room for Miss Bryant? She's going to be with us overnight.'

'Yes, my lady.'

Ava disappeared, just as Jeffreys entered with a silver tray upon which sat a large cup of hot chocolate. Beside it, in two small bowls, were some whipped cream and some tiny marshmallows.

'Thank you.'

'May I get you anything, my lady?' Jeffrey asked the Dowager.

'A whisky, please.'

'Of course, my lady.'

He went over to a drinks cabinet hidden within a large globe and quickly prepared a glass of whisky for the older woman. Then he disappeared again.

It was quite a marvel to experience such service! The closest experience Nell had had to someone serving her was if she sat in a café that had a waitress. To experience proper maid and butler service... It was amazing! But obviously not something that she ought to get used to. Lucas would have loved it... No doubt he would have been pulling on that bellpull to see how quickly someone would arrive.

A cloud must have crossed her face, because suddenly the Dowager was peering at her with interest. 'What's that you're just thinking about?'

'Oh, nothing...'

'Didn't look like nothing.'

The Dowager was astute. Her eyes might be rheumy, but they didn't miss a trick.

'Your grandson mentioned he's a doctor?' said Nell.

'Changing the subject? Okay, then. Yes. He's a children's doctor. A paediatrician.'

Nell had just been taking a sip of her hot chocolate and she felt the hot liquid burn her throat as she swallowed too fast in dismay. A paediatrician! Nell worked on the children's wards. She was specially trained to take blood from children and babies, having trained as a play specialist, too. He was going to be working on *her* wards?

She coughed, trying to clear her throat, her eyes streaming, as she struggled to breathe. They'd been after a new paediatrician for ages, and she'd known he'd be starting today, on her day off.

'And what is it *you* do?' asked the Dowager curiously.

'She's a leech,' said a now familiar voice from across the room.

Nell turned and stared as the man who'd rescued her from the roadside—grandson to the Dowager—entered the room, heading towards his grandmother. The billowing black coat was gone and now she saw a solidly built man, holding a steaming mug, wearing dark jeans and a black fisherman's jumper, stalk-ing across the room. He bent low to drop a kiss upon the older woman's downy, wrinkled cheek, then stood in front of the fire, all tall and brooding, as he warmed his hands.

'A leech?' asked his grandmother.

'He means I'm a phlebotomist. I take people's blood,' she clarified.

'And she also goes out and drives in dangerous weather for no reason,' he mumbled as he sipped at his drink.

She glared at him. 'I was not out for no reason!'

'*Seth!* Is that any way to talk to our guest?'

Seth. So that was his name. Yes. He looked like a Seth. Like an Egyptian god. She could imagine him perfectly, striding about, bare-chested and bare-legged, with gold circlets on his upper arms, emphasising his muscles…

Or was that Set?

She didn't know. Couldn't remember exactly. She was getting confused. And something about him—maybe it was his arrogance—had her feeling…exasperated.

'My apologies,' he said low-voiced, without looking at her.

It didn't sound like an apology at all, and she bristled with a controlled anger that she refused to release out of respect for the fact that she was in someone else's house. A stranger's house. Elmbridge Manor! Certainly not somewhere she belonged.

She stood up, smiled at the Dowager. 'If you'll excuse me? I'll just make another call to my breakdown service.'

'Of course, dear.'

She shot a look at Seth, then left the room to stand in the massive entrance hall with its chequerboard floor.

The breakdown service call-handler—this time a young woman called Lisa—thanked her for her call updating them on her situation, and said that now she was safe and warm they would get someone to her car first thing in the morning, when the storm was expected to have passed.

It wasn't ideal. She had no idea how she would get home. Or even if her car would be rescued by the time she needed it to get to work. But she figured she would just go to her room here and hide away until it was time to leave.

Ending the call, she sucked in a deep breath, relaxed her shoulders and went back into the drawing room.

The Dowager and Seth stopped talking the second she entered.

'So, you're staying the night?' he asked, one black eyebrow raised.

'Yes. Your grandmother was kind enough to offer me a room. But don't worry. I'll be out of your hair by the morning.' Nell settled back into her chair and took a sip of her hot chocolate. It was warm and rich. The perfect sweet antidote to feeling cold.

'Ignore my grandson, dear. He can get grumpy when he hasn't eaten.'

'That's all right. I've dealt with worse,' replied Nell.

She noticed Seth frown.

'Maybe once he's had something to eat Seth could give you a tour? What do you say, Nell?'

'*Nell?*'

She looked at him. 'Yes. That's my name. It's short for Eleanor.'

He smirked. 'I prefer Leech.'

'I think Eleanor is a delightful name—and, again, don't be rude to our guest,' said his grandmother.

Nell smiled her thanks at the Dowager. 'I wouldn't want to bother Seth any more than I already have this evening.'

'Oh, pish! It's no problem at all. Is it, Seth?' the Dowager gave her grandson a look that brooked no argument.

Nell could have sworn she heard him growl.

* * *

He'd returned to Elmbridge Manor to look after his granny on two conditions. One, that he still be allowed to work part-time at the local hospital and two, that she stay out of his life and stop trying to fix him up with ladies she considered to be a good match.

Granny was sweet. Lovely and charming. But after Dana had died she had allowed him a mourning period of one year and then had begun to oh-so-sneakily start arranging things so that he ran into certain available, single, suitable women.

The first had been Lady Sarah Darling. The granddaughter of one of her bridge partners. He'd turned up for his granny's birthday dinner at Elmbridge Manor to find Lady Sarah awaiting him. All glossy-eyed and glossy-lipped. Though he'd tried to be polite, he'd found her dinner conversation about the politics of fashion to be completely uninteresting.

Last year when he'd visited, because his granny had had a fall and broken her hip, he'd found himself being pushed towards the private nurse she'd hired—Laura Jennings— who'd just happened to be the daughter of some business mogul. Granny had hoped that he and Laura would bond over the fact that they were both medics, but thankfully that was not to be. Laura had set him free of any obligation almost immediately by informing him that she knew her granny was trying to set them up together, but was asking him not to bother because she was into girls, not boys.

Happily, they'd enjoyed chatting and being friends, and he'd been let off the hook most gratefully.

He didn't want to be forced into a relationship. He had a lot of baggage. An estate to manage. His inheritance. And a son to look after. A son who'd lost his mother and was still getting used to that. There was absolutely no way in hell he was going to get involved with this Nell woman, no matter how pretty and doe-eyed she was.

The woman was infuriating, for a start. And a risk-taker. Going out in this storm! There was no way he was letting a woman like that anywhere near him or his son. The sooner she left Elmbridge Manor, the better.

Granny had disappeared up to bed, citing tiredness, but he knew her motivations. He'd seen the smile on her face as she'd retired and knew exactly what she was up to. What she was hoping would happen if she left the two of them alone.

Now she'd gone, Nell stood up, facing him.

'You don't have to give me a tour. I don't need it and I'm rather tired, too.'

'Fine. Goodnight.'

He stared back at her. Glad not to be spending any more time with her than was necessary. If she thought he was going to insist on the tour, then she was wrong. Something about her irked him. Whether it was the stupidity of going out in this weather, her argumentative nature, or the rich darkness of her brown eyes, he wasn't sure. Maybe it was all three? He just wanted her gone so he could breathe again.

'You know, you're very rude. I just hope that your bedside manner makes you a much better doctor than you are a human being.'

He took another sip from his coffee, contemplating a sharp retort, but thought better of it. Because each time that she argued with him he felt a stirring within his blood that he didn't want to think too hard about.

He placed his now empty mug on the mantel and looked at her. 'It's late. I'm going to bed.'

Why was he suddenly furnished with images of her laying naked beside him, dark hair splayed over his pillow?

'I trust you'll be gone in the morning.' And he stalked past her, towards the door, thinking he'd reach it and be able to leave without hearing her retort.

Only he wasn't so lucky, and he paused, one hand on the door, as her words reached him.

'Too right. I don't want to stay here a moment longer than I have to.'

Lady Isabel had been carrying the journal until hundreds of photographs on ... newly built ... ... her anger than her eyes.

CHAPTER THREE

THE SEEMINGLY EVER-PRESENT Jeffreys escorted her to her guest room. Following him up the staircase that had caught her eye earlier, she passed portrait after portrait of the Lords Elmbridge and their ladies dressed in sumptuous rich clothes of velvet, silk and lace. The James family. Abraham James... Lady Emilia James... Thomas James...

They all seemed to have the same dark eyes that Seth had, so it felt as if every painting of his ancestors was staring at her and judging her in her torn jeans and the jumper she'd found in a bargain bin at the local charity shop as she passed.

The guest room had a plaque on the door. It was called The Blue Room, apparently, and when Jeffreys opened the door she saw why. The room had dark wood panelling all around, except for the wall that held a small fireplace with a crackling fire going. The carpet was a soft blue, as were the ceiling-to-floor drapes and the counterpane on the bed. The *four-poster* bed. She'd only ever seen those in movies.

Nell remembered to close her mouth quickly enough to turn and thank Jeffreys and wish him a good night.

When he'd closed the door, she'd stared at the bed—and then jumped on it, landing flat on her back, legs and arms splayed as she laughed and chuckled at finding herself in such a marvellous place! She was having a sleepover at Elmbridge Manor!

She stared up at the ceiling, then got up to explore, finding a small en-suite bathroom behind a door that looked like part of the wall. The bathroom had a shower stall, a toilet, and a large, sunken bath in the floor! Maybe she could have a quick wallow in that in the morning before she left?

It would be a shame not to take full advantage of the facilities.

She washed her face and brushed her teeth, with the brand-new toothbrush that she found on the side of the sink in a small marble jar, and then got into bed.

It was extremely comfortable and warm, and as she lay there in the dark, listening to the fire and to the wind still howling outside, she just knew she would have a good night's sleep.

'Goodnight, Lucas,' she said out loud, thinking of her son.

She might not have watched the movie he loved. She might not have eaten the mint choc chip ice cream. But she had managed to visit him. And, believing that he was always with her anyway, she just knew that he would have loved this room and this bed.

'I love you, sweet boy. I miss you. Sweet dreams.'

And she fell fast asleep.

She couldn't remember dreaming, but something woke her early in the morning. A sound?

Her eyes blinked open, adjusting slowly in the dark of the unfamiliar room, until she suddenly sat up with a start at the sight of a ghostly boy standing at the side of her bed, staring down at her, holding a teddy bear against his chest.

'What…? Who are you?'

She reached for the bedside lamp, struggling for the switch, nearly knocking it over in her fright, certain that once the light was on the ghost would go. Or maybe it was part of a dream? Lucas had used to wake her in the middle of the night all the time, and she had been thinking of him before she went to sleep.

But when she turned back the boy still stood there. Golden-haired, but with those same dark eyes she'd seen in Seth and all the James ancestors. Her heart pounded.

'Hello?'

The boy smiled at her. 'Hello. Who are you?'

He was so like Lucas! The colour of his hair… The way it was all mussed up, as if he'd just got out of bed and hadn't combed it yet… It was most unsettling.

'I'm Nell. Who are you?'

And then she heard a voice. Seth's voice. Calling in the corridors outside of her room.

'Olly? Olly?'

She looked at the boy, noticed his brief smile, then he chuckled and ran from the room.

Nell stared after him, her heart thudding strongly in her chest.

'There you are! What were you doing in that room?' she heard Seth say.

She pulled the covers up over her chest and stared at the semi-open door, hoping Seth and the boy would just go away and leave her alone. She didn't need this.

But there was a slight knock on her door and it swung open further. And Seth was suddenly standing there.

He looked just as dark and dangerous as he

had last night. Devilishly so. Did he only have black clothing?

'Did Olly wake you?' he asked.

'Oh... I was awake anyway,' she lied.

He nodded. 'He knows not to wander the corridors and go into people's rooms. I'll have a word with him.'

She stared at him, wondering what his face would look like if he smiled. 'Like I said, I was getting up anyway.'

He didn't look at her. Didn't meet her gaze. Was he just being polite? Not looking at a strange woman whilst she was in bed? Or did he hate her so much that he just couldn't look at her?

'Breakfast is in the morning room. Ring that bell when you're ready and someone will take you.'

And then he was gone again.

Nell let out a breath she hadn't known she'd been holding. Did she really want to go downstairs and share breakfast with that man? Or with that little boy? Olly? Who was he? Seth's son? Some kind of ward? Neither Seth nor his grandmother had mentioned the little boy last night. The topic of conversation had seemed to be her, more than them. Which was fair enough if they were going to let a stranger stay overnight in their home.

She could have been anyone. She could have been a thief and they'd trusted her. Perhaps she ought to be more grateful to Seth, after all? He need not have stopped in that snowy blizzard. He might have driven by and *not* helped. And yet he had, and all they'd given each other since was grief.

Nell got out of bed, performed her morning ablutions, and looked longingly at the sunken bath. But her stomach was rumbling and she knew she needed to go downstairs to thank her hosts for their kindness. And then maybe call the breakdown service again.

Once dressed and presentable, she pulled on the bell and after a minute or two there was a knock at the door.

'Come in!'

Ava stood there. 'You rang, madam?'

'Could you show me to the breakfast room, please? Er…the morning room?'

Ava smiled and nodded. 'Of course, madam. Come with me.'

As they walked along the corridor and down the curving staircase, Nell couldn't help but be intrigued. 'Do you like working here?' she asked the maid.

'I do.'

'And the Dowager and her grandson? They're good employers?'

'The best, madam. Very kind and considerate. They look after all their staff very well.'

Nell raised an eyebrow. She could imagine the Dowager being kind and considerate, but Seth? 'And... Lord Elmbridge?'

She still couldn't get used to the idea that that man was a *lord*. A peer of the realm!

Ava nodded. 'The best. Kind... Considerate... Lord Elmbridge and his grandmother get us birthday gifts each year, and in a few weeks there will be the servants' ball. He and his friends look after us and serve us.' She smiled.

Nell was surprised. She couldn't imagine him being thoughtful and kind at all.

Opening another set of double doors, Ava led Nell into a large room filled with light from all the windows. The walls were a bright daffodil-yellow colour and a long table sat in the middle, set with a fine china and laden with food choices. Cereals. Hot food, like bacon and eggs. Toast. A butter dish and a variety of jams, honeys and marmalades. Croissants. Pastries. Fruit already chopped up and mixed into a fruit salad. Yoghurts. Fruit juices.

'Lord Elmbridge didn't know what you'd like, so he asked us to prepare everything.'

'Oh, right... Well, yes...that is kind.'

'Take a seat, madam.'

'Am I to eat alone?'

'The Dowager will join you in just a few moments.'

'And Lord Elmbridge? And… Olly?'

'They've already eaten. Early risers. Poor little Olly doesn't sleep well since…'

Ava's eyes clouded as she clearly thought better of what she'd been going to say.

'If you need anything, just ring the bell.' She gave a nod of her head, another quick smile, and then she disappeared.

Nell turned back to look at the table groaning under the weight of food. She normally just had toast in the mornings. She couldn't afford much else. But now that all of this was arrayed in front of her… She decided to eat her fill, and began loading a plate with bacon and eggs.

She was halfway through her breakfast when the door opened and the Dowager arrived, smiling and holding onto her cane. 'Good morning, Nell! Did you sleep well, my dear?'

Yes. Until that little boy had startled her. It had been most unsettling to find him in her room. Waking her like Lucas used to. Thank goodness she would never have to endure that ever again!

'I did, thank you. And thanks again for your hospitality. You didn't need to go to so much trouble just for me.'

'Nonsense. We love having guests here. Have you heard any more about your car?'

'I called the breakdown company just a moment ago. My car has been pulled from the ditch and everything still works. Just a new dent in the bonnet and a bit of mud. They're delivering it here. I hope you don't mind?'

'Not at all. We'll be sad to see you go.'

Maybe the Dowager would be—but Seth? She knew he would be glad to see the back of her.

Pixie Ward was the paediatric pre-surgical ward and Nell's favourite. She would often be called there, either to take some bloods or place an IV, or just to help calm a frightened child by distracting them with play activities so that the doctor could examine them.

Some children arrived in quite an unwell state. But Nell knew that on Pixie they would start their journey to being fixed, and that was the very best part for her. Seeing them get better. Seeing them begin to thrive. Smile. Laugh. Seeing the strain leave their parents' faces and waving them goodbye when they all went home.

It was therapy for her. *Good* therapy. Occasionally one of the children would get really sick and they'd have to go off to the PICU—

the paediatric intensive care unit—but mostly her patients' stories had happy endings and that was what she tried to focus on.

Today, she'd been called to attend to a four-year-old girl who was scared of needles. As were her parents, apparently. Nell had been told by the ward sister in charge that though they'd tried, they'd failed after the child got hysterical.

Arriving at the nurses' desk, she smiled at Amy, one of the paediatric nurses, and asked for more on the patient's background.

'Oh, I'm not sure... I've just come on shift and she's a new patient.' Amy looked around. 'No one else is free... Oh! That's her doctor, over there. The new paediatrician guy—Dr James? Maybe ask him?'

Dr James. Lord Elmbridge.

Dread filled her as she turned around to see her grumpy, brooding rescuer heading towards them in dark trousers and a black shirt, with a stethoscope draped around his neck and his hospital ID clipped to his belt.

'Dr James.'

'Leech.' He gave her a smile.

She decided to let that go. 'I'm here to draw blood on Kalisha Smalls. What can you tell me about her?'

He settled into a chair at the desk and began

tapping away at the keyboard. 'Four years of age…brought in due to complications of sickle cell anaemia.'

Sickle cell was a disease that caused blood cells to be of an unusual shape. Because of their sickle shape, they often didn't live as long as normal blood cells, and could also block blood vessels, causing extreme pain and infection.

'She's to undergo a hip arthroplasty after suffering necrosis to her femoral head. We had IVs in situ, as well as a catheter and cannula, but she's pulled them all out. We need them replaced, but she won't let anyone near her, and someone said that you're very good.'

Was that a compliment?

'Oh. Well, that was very kind of "someone" to say. And the parents? What are they like?'

'Extremely needle phobic.'

'Which Kalisha has probably picked up on?'

'I need you to get the IV and cannula back in.' He looked up at her then. Met her gaze. 'Can you do that?'

His eyes were so dark! So mysterious. And yet so cold. Closed off.

'I'll give it my best.'

'That's all I ask.'

She was about to walk away, to go and see

the patient, but she felt she had to say something first. 'I didn't get to see you at breakfast.'

Seth looked up, seemingly annoyed. He was checking around to see who might be listening. Amy was on the phone, talking to a parent and giving an update on their child.

'I was busy.'

Maybe. But she really needed to establish the parameters of their working relationship after the difficulties of how they'd met. Work was her haven and she didn't need to be avoiding anyone.

'I just wanted to say thank you. For helping me out and giving me a place to stay for the evening.'

He was silent for a moment. Then he let out a breath and his face softened. Just a little. 'You're welcome.'

'The young boy... Olly? Is he your son?'

She saw the walls go back up instantly.

'Yes.'

Nell waited for more. But Seth just stared at her. Challenging her, almost.

Wow... This guy was a paediatrician? Most paediatric doctors she met were warm and kind. Sometimes a little silly, so they could engage with their patients. This man was... Well. There wasn't a word for what this man was. Except maybe *Lord*. Someone who looked down on everyone else.

'And?' he asked.

She smiled. Why did she bother? Why bother trying to get to know him? He wouldn't be staying.

'And nothing. I'll go and see Kalisha.'

He hadn't meant to be so prickly, but there was something about Nell that made him feel on edge, and when she'd started asking him about Olly…the boy he felt he'd failed…he'd instantly felt under attack. Maybe he didn't need to be so defensive, but he wanted to protect Olly as much as he could, and he wasn't going to have her criticising him. He did enough of that himself.

So when had Nell looked at him as if she wanted to kill him, just before she'd stalked away, he'd let out a breath and run his hands through his hair in exasperation. He'd been rude. He could admit that. And if he and Nell were going to have to work with one another then maybe he ought to offer some sort of olive branch?

He loved his job. Loved interacting with his patients. He felt at home on the wards. This was a place where he felt in control and that he knew what he was doing. He didn't need it to become a battlefield.

Seth finished typing his notes, updating a patient's drug chart, and then decided to go and see Nell at work with Kalisha. See what made her so special and the phlebotomist of choice for Pixie Ward, whose praises everyone sang in perfect harmony.

Kalisha was in a six-bed ward. The walls were decorated with a mural that made it look as if the children were in a land full of pixies. There were flowers and mushrooms, all of which were homes for pixies that seemed to have been caught in a snapshot of their lives. One purple pixie was holding a small basket filled with flowers and fruits, another pixie, this time in pink, was listening to music and pirouetting in a dance beneath a large daisy, and by Kalisha's bed a pixie lay on her tummy, by a pond, watching all the fish swimming below.

Nell was by the bed, smiling and laughing with the parents.

Seth decided to watch.

Nell began talking to Kalisha. 'So, I hear you're a very brave girl and going to have an operation?'

Kalisha nodded shyly, clutching onto her teddy bear.

'Does anything hurt, my lovely?'

The little girl nodded.

'Can you point to where it hurts?'

Kalisha pointed to her left hip.

'I bet it does! You poor thing… I'd really like to help take your pain away. Would you like that?'

Another nod.

'Well, we can give you some magic medicine that will do that.'

'She doesn't like needles,' said Kalisha's mother.

Nell smiled. 'I know.'

Seth watched with interest.

'See this little cup of juice here, that the nurse brought earlier? That will help take away some of your pain. All you have to do is drink it.'

'I don't want to,' said Kalisha in a small voice.

'Oh, honey, why not? Do you think it'll taste bad? It doesn't. It tastes of strawberries—do you like strawberries?'

'I do…'

'She's worried that it will put her to sleep and she'll wake up with needles in her again,' said the mother.

'Well, I can see why you'd be upset about that, Kalisha. I wouldn't want that, either. Not without my permission.'

Seth frowned. They had already told Kalisha that when she came round from her surgery there would be tubes and wires in her arms, and how important it was that they stay there.

'But what you had in your arms weren't actually needles. They were just very small tubes, helping keep you well before your surgery. You've been through a lot, huh?'

The little girl nodded.

'And those little tubes? Well, we need to put them back if we're to make you better. They help us give you medicine to take away that pain. And you want to feel better, don't you? So you can go home?'

'Yes…'

'How about I promise to do that for you and you won't feel a thing?'

'But needles hurt.'

'Not with my magic cream, they don't. Here, let me show you. No needles, just cream— okay?'

Kalisha let her put some cream on the back of one of her hands.

'We'll let that sit there for a moment and do its magic. Hey, do you like bubbles?'

Kalisha smiled and nodded.

Seth watched as Nell got out a bubble wand from her bag and began blowing bubbles for Kalisha to reach out and touch. Then she passed the wand and the mixture to the little girl, to play with herself.

A smile crept onto his face as he watched Nell with the little girl. She was good. He had to give her that. She used words that were easy for a four-year-old to understand, and hadn't been patronising nor talked down to her at all. Nell had talked to her as if her very real concerns were extremely valid and he liked that.

After a short period of time during which bubbles filled the ward, Nell suggested that she wipe away the magic cream.

'And now I'm going to touch your skin where the cream was. Can you feel me touching you?'

Kalisha looked at her in amazement. 'I can't feel it! Mummy, I can't feel it!' She laughed.

'That's good. You see! So if you'll let me put the tubes back in, we can use this cream and you won't feel a thing. And if you like, whilst I do it, you can blow bubbles and look at Mummy and Daddy and have fun, and you won't have to worry about anything at all. And afterwards, you'll feel so much better. How does that sound?'

'You promise?'

'Cross my heart.' Nell made a crossing motion over her chest.

Kalisha looked at her mum and then her dad.

'Want me to do Teddy first?' Nell asked.

After a quick nod from Kalisha, Nell put a dot of magic cream on the teddy, then gathered her things, wiped off the cream and inserted an IV into the toy.

'See? Your turn now. Are you ready to be a twin with Teddy?'

'His name's Toby.'

Nell smiled. 'I love that name. So…are you ready? Here's the bubbles. You look at Mummy and Daddy and I'll be done faster than you can say lickety-split.'

Kalisha began blowing bubbles, looking away from her.

Seth could see Nell would need to work fast. But she had gained Kalisha's trust and that was the most important thing. He was impressed. Nell's reputation was true. And when she got the IV in first time, all hooked up without Kalisha even flinching, he knew he was in the presence of a master.

'There you go. All done.'

Nell watched as Kalisha looked at her arm.

'I didn't even feel it go in.'

'Magic cream!' Nell laughed. 'Now, remember, it's not a needle in your arm—just a small bendy tube. So you can use your arm as normal, okay?'

'Okay.'

'Will you and Toby be all right?'

'We will. Now we're twins.'

'Good.'

Nell got up and turned around, and saw him standing there in the doorway, watching.

Was that a blush he saw? he wondered.

Interesting.

As she moved towards him, carrying her kit, he stood up straight.

'That was good…what you just did.'

She shrugged. 'It's just my job—nothing more.'

He smiled. 'I'm giving you a compliment.'

'Oh. Well, I didn't recognise it because I didn't know you could say nice things.'

'I say nice things. On occasion. When they're merited.'

'Noted. Do you need me for anything?'

No. He didn't. But he wasn't ready for her to go yet, strangely. What was it about Nell Bryant that intrigued him so? Her spiky nature? The way she couldn't give two hoots about who he was or where he lived? Most people upon finding out who he was would suddenly change and become obsequious, which he hated. So the fact that she didn't… He kind of liked it. Kind of liked their argumentative banter. It was fun.

'How's your car?' he asked.

'Dented. Muddy. But working.'

'Good.'

'How are your reindeer?' She laughed. 'That's not a sentence I ever thought I'd say.'

'Safely contained. We found the last one.'

Maybe it was her eyes? She had nice eyes. Dark. Chocolatey…

She stared at him, as if trying to figure him out. Then she frowned. 'Okay, then.'

And she walked past him to the nurses' desk to add her procedure to Kalisha's chart.

He watched her go, realised he was admiring her pert behind, and then instantly turned away. He had a post-surgical check to do—best to get on with that and stop thinking about Nell Bryant.

Not her eyes, nor her behind.

CHAPTER FOUR

'So, THE NEW DOCTOR—Dr James. What do we think?' asked Beth, one of the nurses, as they sat together in their lunch hour.

There were four of them. Beth, Nell, a healthcare assistant called Lou and another nurse, Angel.

Nell had plenty to say on the subject of Dr Seth James, but she was intrigued to hear what the others thought.

'I think he's hot,' said Angel. 'He's got that dangerous, devil-may-care look about him. All rough and ready. He looks like he'd be good in bed, right?'

The others made appreciative noises.

'He looks like a real man. Solid. Strong. You can tell he's fit,' said Lou.

'I think he looks like a pirate,' said Beth. 'That dark hair and that dark beard... You'd expect him to wear a gold hoop earring and have a parrot on his shoulder… I mean, swoon alert—am I right?'

Nell felt as if they were waiting for her to agree. 'You don't think he's a little…standoffish?' she asked.

They all turned to look at her as if she were crazy.

'No! Not at all. What makes you say that?'

'He just… I mean, he…' She could feel herself getting flustered.

All the things the other girls had said were true. Dr James *was* very attractive, in that rough and ready kind of way, but she felt she'd seen a side of him that they hadn't.

'You know he's a lord, right?'

'A lord? Of what?'

'Like a real lord…a peer and a landowner.'

'You mean he sent off for one of those certificates where you own a tiny scrap of land in Scotland and you become a laird, or something?'

'No.' She shook her head. 'He's Lord Elmbridge. Of Elmbridge Manor.'

They all looked at one another in surprise.

'Well, knock me down with a feather… Should we curtsey?' asked Beth, laughing. 'How do you know this?'

Nell didn't want to tell them what had happened. Not at all. 'I just heard, that's all.' She must have blushed, because suddenly they were all pointing at her.

'Come on! Spill! You know more than you're letting on!'

'I swear, that's it. That's all I know.'

At that very moment, the Lord in question walked into the hospital cafeteria, grabbed a tray and began to line up for some food.

Beth pointed. 'He's here! Do you think he knows how to serve himself?'

'Who cares?' Angel laughed. 'Let's just take a few moments to enjoy his rear view.'

The girls sighed and chuckled, but Nell didn't know where to look. She regretted telling them he was a lord, but she'd been stuck for something to say, and to take the pressure off herself—not wanting to admit that she did indeed find him very attractive—she'd presented the group with a tasty morsel of information.

Now, unable to resist as everyone gawped at Seth, she looked up and risked a glance.

He was very fine indeed. All that they had said and more. And maybe that was the problem? Or an added problem, seeing as he didn't seem to like her very much. Not that that mattered. Nell wasn't looking for a relationship. With anyone.

Why would she risk getting involved in something like that again? She'd only end up getting hurt and left behind, her heart in tatters and shreds, held together by scars and pain. And Dr Seth James, or Lord Elmbridge, or whatever it was he wanted to be called, would never, ever—not in a million years—be the man for her.

Never.

So why was she still looking at him? Why was she still engaged in noting those wide, broad shoulders in a tight-fitting, surely bespoke black shirt? Looking at the way his dark, almost black hair curled around the collar? And why did she note, with appreciation, the neatness and flatness of his waist? And why on earth was she admiring the curve of his backside in those dark jeans?

Flustered, she took a bite of her sandwich and deliberately looked away. She would not be caught gazing at him when he turned around. She would not give him the satisfaction, even if everyone else was clucking like a gaggle of hens around a new... *Ahem*. Male chicken.

'So, what's everyone doing for Christmas?' she asked.

'Well, not *him*, sadly.' Lou chuckled. 'I'm off to the outlaws. What about you?'

And just like that her friends were distracted into talking about Christmas plans.

Nell had none. As usual. Christmas was

something that she never really wanted to bother with any more, but she still decorated, still bought a turkey with all the trimmings and made dinner on Christmas Day, because it was what Lucas would have wanted. It was what Lucas had loved. By doing so it brought him closer, and she would take that over anything.

'Me, too,' said Beth.

'Me three,' said Angel.

'Dinner for one,' Nell said, smiling a smile that said, *Don't feel sorry for me.* 'As usual.'

'Maybe you should have Christmas with the Lord?' suggested Beth. 'There's no ring on his finger. Maybe he's single?'

'Looking like that?' said Lou. 'There's no way that man is on his own.'

Seth sat in the hospital cafeteria, trying to eat the chilli con carne and jacket potato that he'd selected from the hot food section. He noticed Nell Bryant the phlebotomist on the other side of the room, sitting with a group of friends.

Her hair was down, and as the winter sun shone in through the window behind her it gleamed and shimmered, revealing hidden streaks of red and copper amongst the dark brown as it fell in waves down her back.

He looked away and pulled out his phone, determined not to spend more time than was necessary thinking about or noticing Nell. Nothing could ever come of it. He had bigger priorities right now. Looking after Granny and Olly. Getting into running the manor as a business. And he wanted to make Christmas really special this year for his son.

The last couple of Christmases had been hard, down in Devon, but he'd told himself it was easier to be away from where the accident had happened. Olly had missed his mother intensely—still did, no doubt—only as more and more time passed his pain didn't show as much, and he'd felt that it was the right time to return to Elmbridge.

It was his childhood home, and it always felt good to return there. Even if it did bring back memories of Dana's accident and alongside that all his regrets. His guilt. His shame.

If only he hadn't wanted to enjoy a drink at that Christmas party...

If only he hadn't let Dana offer to collect him and bring him home...

If only...

If only...

Without realising what he was doing, he let his gaze drift back over to Nell. She was laughing now, enjoying a joke or something, and he was amazed at how her face lit up with her smile. He'd not seen that yet. Not a true smile.

He'd seen her sarcastic one, but it was nothing compared to this. Genuine. Warm. Her doe eyes gleaming with mirth and enjoyment. He wondered if he'd ever get to make her smile like that. What would it feel like to make her smile and know he was the reason for it?

His phone beeped, dragging him from his reverie. It was a text from Sven, to let him know that the delivery of hay for the reindeer had arrived, as expected. He texted back. And then a text arrived from his grandmother, reminding him that tonight Santa's Grotto would officially open and he was to be there at six sharp to cut the candy-cane-striped ribbon.

Part of him rued the day he'd taught his grandmother how to text. The other part actually liked it. Granny, apart from Olly, was all he had left of his family, and she was like a cat with nine lives. Every time she got sick, or hurt, she'd end up in hospital and he'd worry he was going to lose her—only for her to bounce back.

One day, he knew she wouldn't. And then he'd miss her texts and her love. So he smiled, and messaged back that he would be there on time, and that, no, he hadn't forgotten.

He suddenly became aware of a presence beside his table. He looked up. 'Leech...' He smiled.

Her head tilted to one side as she rolled her eyes. 'You could just call me Nell, like everyone else, you know.'

'But where would the fun be in that?'

'Perhaps I should come up with a name for you?'

'Like what?'

She shrugged. 'I don't know… My Lord? Lord Grumpy?'

'They're not very inventive, are they? Aren't you embarrassed?'

'Well, I'm trying to be polite. They're not the first names I came up with for you.'

'Which were…?'

'Well, let's just say they were a whole slew of swear words.'

'That's rather mean…and not really in the spirit of Christmas. Don't you think?'

'Since when have *you* been in the spirit of Christmas?'

He smiled and got to his feet, towering over her. 'As always, it's a pleasure talking with you, Leech, but I have things to be getting on with. I'm a very busy person.'

'As am I.'

'I'm sure you are. Enjoy your day.'

He grabbed his tray and returned it, and then headed out of the cafeteria back towards the ward. He felt confused. He enjoyed their banter. Enjoyed baiting her. And at the same time he found himself drawn to her. His eyes sought her out in places, almost as if they were out of his control—which was ridiculous, because his body was his own and he felt sure his brain was in charge, and not something lower.

So why did he keep running into her?

As he'd said to her before, it was a large hospital. They might never run into one another.

And yet they did.

Over and over again.

Nell was feeling mightily annoyed with Lord Grumpy after their encounter in the hospital cafeteria. She'd only gone over to tell him that she'd accidentally let it slip that he was a lord to her friends, but the conversation had not been what she'd expected. He was still calling her Leech, which was funny in one way and annoying in another. She kind of liked it that he had a nickname for her, and that they could argue without it actually being mean, but she didn't like the feeling that he had somehow bested her.

So when she got back to Pixie Ward and overheard Paula, the ward sister, on the phone, talking about how their usual Santa couldn't visit the wards to give gifts to the children who'd be stuck there over Christmas, she had a wonderful idea.

She waited for the ward sister's conversation to be over, then knocked with her knuckles on the door. 'Hi. Couldn't help but overhear about Gordon. What's happened to him?'

'Broke his hip after falling over in that snow we had at the weekend. So we need to find another Santa fast.'

Nell smiled. 'I have one in mind… I'm sure he'd love to do it.'

The ward sister perked up. 'Oh? Who?'

'Dr James! He loves Christmas! He was just telling me. And he's only part-time, so he could do it. I'm sure he wouldn't want to let the children down.'

'Do you think he would?'

'I'm sure he would if you asked him. I believe he's even got his own reindeer.'

She didn't explain when Paula raised an eyebrow at that. Maybe she'd think Nell meant he had a collection of reindeer. As in ornaments.

The more she thought about it, the more it seemed to her that Dr James was perfect! He had reindeer. His own Santa's Grotto, which the Dowager had told her about. And it would be hilarious, seeing him all dressed up in a Santa outfit and a white beard, ho-ho-ho-ing with the children and having to be happy and cheery. She'd get a real kick out of it…maybe even make him pose for a photo or two.

'Okay. I'll ask him. Know where hc is?'

'He should be on the ward somewhere.'

Paula stood up and smiled. 'Perfect! I'll go and find him. Thanks, Nell.'

'You're very welcome.'

Nell went to see her next patient feeling rather pleased with herself, imagining the look on Lord Grumpy's face when Paula tracked him down. She couldn't imagine that he'd be able to get out of it. How did you say no to a determined ward sister who needed a Santa for her ward?

Daniel Cohen was a ten-year-old boy who was in for a liver surgery and needed a liver function test, group and save, as well as a full blood count before his operation. He was a charming young man. Very polite even though jaundiced-looking. Hopefully once he'd had his surgery he'd be back to his normal self again.

'Hey, Daniel. I'm here to take some of your blood. How are you with needles?'

'Do they hurt?'

'No. I have magic cream. Want to see?'

Daniel nodded.

Nell placed a splodge of cream on the back

of his hand, covered it with a dressing, and drew a happy smiling face on top.

'In a minute or two you won't be able to feel anything there. So, tell me, Daniel, when you're not in hospital, what do you like doing?'

'Playing football. But my parents have stopped me since I got sick. They say it's too dangerous for me.'

'You must miss it?'

'Yeah.'

'Who do you support?'

As Daniel went into a long answer about his favourite club and his favourite players, Nell removed the dressing and the cream and showed him that the crook of his elbow was now numb. She inserted the needle without any trouble at all, and got the blood draw.

'See? All done. Want a sticker?'

She opened her packet of stickers and he picked one with a green dragon on it that said he'd been brave today.

'Thanks. Are you in trouble?' he asked.

Nell frowned and looked at him with a smile. 'Trouble? No. Why do you say that?'

'Because that man behind you is looking at you funny.'

Nell turned to see Dr James standing at the foot of Daniel's bed, arms crossed.

She blushed. 'Dr James.'

He forced a smile for Daniel. 'Might I have a word with you, Miss Bryant?'

She stood up, knowing what this was about and rather looking forward to hearing him bluff and curse and bluster about how she'd set him up to be the ward Santa.

'Of course,' she answered, all sweet and innocent, as they headed away from the ward and into the corridor. She looked up at him, all smiles. 'What can I do for you?'

But instead of the anger and irritation she'd expected, he disarmed her and smiled. 'You may have heard... I'm going to be the ward Santa this year.'

'I might have heard something.'

Another smile—but this one was dangerous. 'I was honoured to be asked, being so new to the ward, and I told Paula I'd be pleased to do it. But I might need an assistant to help me. An elf assistant.'

The pleasure in his eyes told her exactly where this was heading.

'I can't be an—'

'Oh, but you can! There's even an elf costume for you. Paula's dug it out and I think you'll like it. It's very...fetching. We're going to be the perfect partnership.'

Nell stared at him in horror. Be his elf? His assistant? Spend hours with him trailing around the wards, being the butt of his jokes? It was going to be impossible!

'I can't.'

'You would let down the *children*?' he asked in a soft voice of mock horror, his arms crossed over his chest as he leaned casually against the wall.

No. She would not let down the children. She would be his elf just to spite him.

'Fine. I'll be your elf.'

'I knew you would.'

'I should have known you wouldn't be able to do it without a servant!'

He chuckled in amusement. 'And I should have known that *you* would do the unexpected. But I think I'm getting to know you now, Little Elf. And you and I are going to be very close from now on, because it's the only way I'm going to be able to keep an eye on you.'

He gave her a wink and walked away.

What have I done?

She thought she'd played a prank on him. Thought she'd got one up on him after the rude way he'd spoken to her in the cafeteria, calling her Leech. Now it seemed she had a new name. Little Elf was nicer than Leech, but he seemed to have the upper hand here. But he would, wouldn't he? He'd been born into it.

And no matter what she tried, she'd never pull him down a peg or two.

Dr Seth James was the most infuriating man she had ever had the misfortune to meet!

CHAPTER FIVE

THE OPENING OF the grotto went really well. Seth cut the ribbon, posed next to Santa and his elves for a photograph for the local newspaper, then stood by and talked to the journalists who wanted quotes for their articles as parents lined up with their children to see Santa.

But he wasn't used to being in the limelight like this. It wasn't something he sought out. It was why he stayed away from Elmbridge, usually. His other home was in Devon, on the south coast. A nice little cottage, tucked away against a rock face, where he and Olly could live their lives and just be like everyone else.

He'd returned to Elmbridge because of his grandmother. Because she'd asked. Because she'd told him the time was coming closer when he would have to be the Lord Elmbridge he'd always been meant to be and that Olly needed to know about his history and his heritage.

She was right. Elmbridge would be Olly's one day. And so he'd come back as soon as he'd secured the hospital position. He was lucky in that money was no object. But he couldn't *not* work. He loved being a paediatrician.

Children were so honest. So open. That was why he'd agreed to open a grotto in the grounds of the Manor this year with no charge, so any child could see Santa. And it was why he'd agreed to be the ward Santa when the sister had told him that Nell had volunteered his name.

Nell Bryant.

She was a funny one, that was for sure. Okay, so they hadn't got off to the best start with one another, but now he felt as if it had become a series of small battles between them, and he had to admit he was beginning to enjoy it. But there was no way he was going to let her get the better of him. She'd thought she'd wind him up by volunteering his name and that he'd say no. So of course he'd had to sidestep that and do the complete opposite! Plus he'd have fun doing it. His Little Elf was going to rue the day she'd ever messed with him.

Amadi Babangida was a seven-year-old boy who had been admitted for surgery on his twisted foot. He had been born in Nigeria with the deformity, and a charity had arranged for him to be brought over to the UK to have the surgery that would straighten it and allow him to walk without crutches. His metatarsals and ankle joint would need pinning, with plates and screws to straighten the foot and allow him to bear weight on it, as so far he could not.

Amadi was a cheerful young boy, who had travelled over with an aunt. His mother had stayed at home with her other four children.

'How are you doing, Amadi?' asked Seth, standing by his bed.

'Okay.'

'Nervous? It's a big day today.'

'But I will be better after.'

'That's right. Not only better, but awesome! We'll have you up and walking in no time!'

'And playing football? And cricket?' Amadi asked with a light in his eyes.

'Absolutely!' Seth looked him over. 'Let me guess…fast bowler?'

Amadi nodded, his teeth gleaming in his bright smile. 'Do you play?'

'I haven't played cricket since I was your age. Rugby was always my game. So, Mrs Chiagozie, do you have any questions?'

Amadi's aunt smiled and shook her head.

'Okay. Well, we've got an hour or two before Amadi goes to Theatre, so if you do think of anything you want to ask, then grab a nurse and someone can come and find me. I'm not a surgeon, so I'm always here—okay?'

A nod.

Seth held out his hand and shook Amadi's. 'See you soon.'

'See you.'

He gave the boy one last winning smile, winked at him, and then headed to a side room to check on a patient who had spiked a fever before her planned surgery and then developed a cough. Concerned about Covid, the nursing staff had isolated her, and he was going in to tell the parents the bad news.

Once he was gowned, gloved and masked, he entered the room and looked at the parents, before settling his gaze on Holly, his patient.

'You've tested positive for Covid, I'm afraid, Holls, so we're going to have to postpone the tonsillectomy until you're better. But because your fever is quite high we're going to keep you in and transfer you to another ward to keep an eye on you. How do you feel about that?'

Holly coughed hard. 'I don't know...'

'Is she going to be all right?' asked her dad.

'Kids are resilient. We'll keep a close watch on her...try and keep that fever down.'

'Will it affect her tonsils? She already suffers so much.'

'It could aggravate them. But, like I say, we'll keep a lookout for any complications.'

'Whatever's best. But it is disappointing. We were hoping to finally be rid of the damn things. They've been trouble for her ever since she was born.'

'I get that, and I know it's hard to wait, but it's safer to do the operation when she doesn't have Covid.'

Both parents nodded and the mother reached out to squeeze her daughter's hand. 'Where will she be moved to?'

'We have a paediatric Covid ward. It's best for us to put her there…just because her oxygen saturations have been up and down.'

'Is that bad?'

'It's not ideal. We like them to be over ninety-four, and Holly's have been dropping into the eighties. We'll give her some oxygen therapy too—get her feeling better.'

He understood the parents' frustrations. No one wanted an operation to be cancelled. You'd build yourself up for it, get mentally prepared, and then for it to not happen… But there was nothing they could do. It would be safer to operate when Holly was Covid-free and maintaining better oxygen levels.

'When will she be moved?' asked the father.

'Soon. We have to take some precautions

when moving a positive Covid case through the hospital.'

The parents and Holly nodded, before Hollt coughed once again. Seth told them he'd come and see them later, when Holly was settled on her new ward, and then left, removing his PPE and depositing it in a special collection bin. Then he washed his hands and checked his watch.

It was time for him to go and see if this Santa costume would fit him. The usual Santa was considerably shorter than Seth, so he needed to know if there were any problems. If there were, he'd simply buy a new Santa outfit. It might even be fun. He could wear it for Olly, too.

But as he headed down the corridor towards the bank of lifts he saw Nell coming his way. She was on her mobile. Smiling. Laughing. Catching her like that, in a spontaneous moment before she noticed him was nice. She looked good...he couldn't deny that. Those dark waves were tied up and out of the way now, but she had allowed some longer tresses to come loose and frame her heart-shaped face.

And then she noticed him, and he watched as her face and posture changed. It was as if she'd gone on the alert as she ended her call, snapped her phone shut and placed it in her pocket.

'Dr James.'

'Little Elf.'

She rolled her eyes. 'I told you before… It wouldn't hurt you to call me Nell.'

He smiled. 'I know. But it annoys you when I don't, so why don't we stick with that?'

'Okay. Fine!' she said, as if it didn't really matter. 'Are you done for the day? On your way back to your palatial mansion?'

'Santa costume fitting.'

'Ah, yes. You're going to look marvellous with a big, fat belly and a bushy white beard.'

'You like beards?' he asked, stroking his own dark one.

'I read something quite interesting about them the other day, actually.'

'Oh? Pray tell.'

'That a beard is not linked to testosterone levels at all. Women like men who are clean-shaven as well as bearded, so men don't grow one to attract a mate.'

'So, what's the reason?'

She smiled. 'They do it because men with beards are perceived as older, wiser and more aggressive than other males. It's science. A beard is meant to be intimidating, to frighten weaker males away from the available females. Interesting, don't you think? That in an evolutionary way you're nothing more than a peacock, trying to look more impressive than other men.'

He laughed, amused by her suggestion. 'I'm not competing with anybody. I happen to like how it looks. That's all.'

Nell smiled. 'You keep telling yourself that.'

And she passed him by, heading towards Pixie Ward.

He narrowed his eyes as he watched her walk away. Her hips drew his gaze and he shook his head as he thought about what she'd just said. He was no peacock! He felt no need to display his feathers and have others admire him. He needed no one's admiration, and nor did he look for it. All he wanted was to be a good dad for Olly. It was just, what with the manor, and working at the hospital, he'd forgotten to shave. Sometimes he was so tired he didn't have the energy for it, and had figured the beard would have to do. And now he liked how it looked, that was all.

At least it had grown through the same dark colour as the hair on his head. He remembered his father having dark, almost black hair, but his beard, when he had grown one, had come through auburn. With his greying eyebrows, he'd looked mismatched, as if put together by a child, so after that he'd kept himself clean-shaven every day, no matter what.

Seth's father had died young. A sudden heart attack that no one had seen coming. He'd grown up without a father and then, a couple of years later, without a mother. He remembered his childhood as being empty and strange, being raised by a granny who did her best, but…

Now Olly had no mother. And Seth was determined to be the best father he could for his son. And if that meant lying on the floor, playing with cars or blocks or doing jigsaws, rather than shaving his beard, then that was what he was going to do! Little Elf could come up with as many crazy theories as she liked, but he knew none of them were true.

He was trying to be a good dad and that was all that mattered.

The dreaded day had arrived.

Elf Day.

It wasn't Christmas yet. There were still a few more days. But on Pixie Ward Santa made visits early—and if Santa was doing his rounds, then he would need his elf, too.

Nell stood in the staff room, staring at the outfit with which she'd been provided. She had to wear that? In front of *him*? This was just going to give him a whole other level of ammunition to torment her with.

When she was finished dressing, she stared at herself in the mirror.

Soft red velvet shoes with jingle bells on curled over her toes. Green-and-white-striped tights. A red tunic and breeches. A green hat with more jingle bells.

Behind her, the door opened and in walked Beth. 'Oh, wow! You look…'

'Stupid?'

'*Festive* was the word I was going for.' Beth stood behind her, peering into the mirror, too. 'Mind you, I feel like there's something missing…'

'Missing? Are we looking at the same reflection?'

'I know!' Beth rummaged in her own locker and pulled out her make-up bag. She turned Nell to face her. Then she drew a large red spot on both her cheeks and, using an eyeliner pencil, added freckles over them. 'There. Perfect!'

Nell felt ridiculous, but had to admit the kids would probably love it—despite her own misgivings.

Beth snapped a couple of pictures on her phone and passed it to her. 'So you remember?'

'Remember what?'

'That Lucas would have loved this. Seeing his mum being silly.'

It was true, and it made her smile. She could

do that now. Once upon a time she hadn't been able to hear his name or be reminded of him without breaking down into a weeping mess. But now...? Now she could think of him happily.

She'd not had him in her life long. Only four years. But she'd known him inside out. What he loved. What made him laugh. What made him seek her out in the middle of the night.

Lucas had often had wild and crazy dreams, and when they'd woken him he'd ambled into her room, holding on to his teddy bear, so he could tell her about them. And then she'd invited him into her bed, and they'd snuggled together for a while before they both fell asleep.

Her husband hadn't liked it. He was a man who believed that children should stay in their own beds, in their own rooms. But perhaps if he'd known how short a time they'd actually have Lucas he might have allowed it, instead of arguing with her about it all the time? Did Blake regret it? All his rules? His regulations? His firm belief that babies ought to be left to cry themselves to sleep? That they shouldn't be in their parents' bed? That breastfeeding should end at six months?

She and Blake had had so many arguments about so many silly things, when what they ought to have been doing was soaking up every millisecond they had with their son. But Blake had always been standoffish. Nell had put it down to the way he'd been raised as a child himself. His parents had been cold. Only showing love through buying their son gifts, rather than giving him hugs and kisses.

When Blake had walked away after Lucas died it had seemed easier for him to get over the loss. She'd never seen him cry. Not even at the funeral. His face stoic. Stone-like. That was what they'd argued about. How unfeeling he'd seemed when all Nell had wanted was for him to hold her and tell her they'd get through this.

And they had.

Just not together.

'You know, I put pictures like this in a giant folder on the computer...as if I'm still saving memories for him.'

Beth looked at her with a soft smile. 'That's nice. You should.'

'He'll never get to see them, though, will he?'

'No. But the children you see today will see you. And they'll remember Santa and his elf visiting them that time they were in hospital. You'll be in those children's memory their entire life.'

'You're right. And I want to make this special for them. Jingle bells and all.'

She lifted a foot and jiggled it. The bells sounded and they both smiled.

'Where's your Santa?'

'Getting changed in the men's changing rooms.'

Beth laughed. 'Now, *there's* a man who could rummage in my stocking.'

Nell raised an eyebrow. 'I don't know... I can't imagine him being...*romantic*, can you?'

'I don't need romance with a man who looks like him. Just getting down and dirty would do it!'

At that moment the door to the men's changing area opened. The first thing that emerged was Santa's giant belly, clad in his familiar red suit, and then the rest of him.

'Ho-ho-ho! Merry Christmas!' Seth said in a deep voice, eyes twinkling as he carried his large sack of presents behind him.

The gifts had all been donated. Collected throughout the year, wrapped by hospital volunteers and kept ready for the festive season.

He stopped to admire Nell. 'My, don't you look jolly?'

'So do you! And here was me thinking that the only character you could play convincingly would be Ebenezer Scrooge. Are you ready to put some smiles on children's faces, or would you prefer to stay here and count all your money?'

He sidled up to her and pulled down the long, white curly beard that covered his own. 'Oh, I don't know… Just putting on the red suit makes me want to make people happy. Even you, Little Elf. What do you say?'

The fact that he'd chosen not to wind her up surprised her. 'All right. Maybe you ought to always wear it, if it makes you nicer.'

'Well, only good boys and girls get what they want for Christmas. Tell me, Little Elf, have you been a good girl?'

She coloured under the intensity of his gaze. The Santa hat, padded belly and fake beard ought to have made him look a figure of ridicule, but he managed to pull it off and be ridiculously sexy. It was annoying!

'I'm always a good girl. How about you?'

He smiled and raised the beard back up. 'Now, that would be telling. Come on!'

And he began to walk out of the staff room.

Nell looked at Beth with a look that said *Can you believe this guy?* Only to see her friend and colleague staring at her in surprise.

'What?' she asked.

'Are you and he…?' Beth trailed off.

'Are he and I what?'

Beth grinned. 'Flirting?'

'Absolutely not!'

'Are you sure?'

'Most definitely!'

'Well, honey, maybe you ought to tell the rest of you. And him. Because that…? What I just saw…? That was the very definition of two people flirting with one another.'

'You're crazy. He's the most annoying man I've ever had the misfortune to meet.'

'Little Elf!'

They heard his voice calling from the corridor.

'Oh, sweetie… You're in trouble with a capital T.'

Nell frowned at her friend, wanting to retort, to dismiss what Beth had suggested, but there were no words in her brain.

Exasperated, she simply said, 'Bah, humbug!' and stalked from the room.

Seth was having enormous fun as Santa. Normally at the hospital he had to keep a professional distance with his young patients. It protected him for when things went badly—as they sometimes did. But as Santa he wasn't at their bedside as a doctor, advising them on pain management or talking through surgery with a parent. He could be as jolly as he wanted! As friendly as he wanted! And it was so wonderful to see the smiles he put on the young kids' faces.

The next kid he was visiting was Peyton Swan. A young girl on the post-surgical ward who had been in to have a meningioma removed from her brain.

Her first visit to the hospital had been when she was three years old, to have the tumour removed then, but due to its positioning they hadn't been able to get it all. So she came in every couple of years to have more taken out. She was now seven, and this was her third surgery. She lay in bed, her head wrapped in thick bandages, looking pale and tired.

'Peyton Swan! Ho-ho-ho! It is so good to see you again! How are you doing?' Seth asked in his jolly Santa voice.

'I'm okay...' she answered in a quiet voice.

'I've brought someone special with me this year. One of my elves from the North Pole. Little Elf, say hello to Peyton!'

Nell stepped forward with a jingle and took hold of Peyton's limp hand. 'Nice to meet you, Peyton!'

Seth grinned behind his fake beard. 'Have you been a good girl this year?'

Peyton nodded shyly.

'Good! I'm glad to hear it! Good boys and girls get presents for Christmas! What have you wished for this year?' Seth was now kneeling beside the bed.

Peyton was thoughtful for a moment. 'To not have to come into hospital any more.'

He got that. She'd already been through so much. Her childhood so far had been spent in and out of hospitals and recovering from brain surgeries. Had this young girl ever had the chance to go skating? Or to ride a pony? Or go to gymnastics class?

He knew she would not get her wish. Peyton faced a lifetime of maintenance surgeries. She would be constantly coming in to hospital to have the growing tumour cut away in order to maintain her quality of life.

'I hear you, Peyton. I really do.' Seth reached for her hand and squeezed it. 'But that's up to the doctors. I may be Santa, but I don't have a magic wand to take your tumour away from you. The only thing I can do is to try and make you smile and be happy…if only for a little while.'

He hated feeling helpless. Hated it that he couldn't make her feel better. But he was not a surgeon. He didn't know the true extent of her case.

'So tell me…what can I do right now to make you smile?'

The little girl thought for a moment more. 'Sing for me?'

He smiled. 'You like singing and music?'

'I do.'

'What song would you like us to sing?'

'The one about Rudolph the reindeer.'

Seth nodded. 'Ah, Rudolph...my favourite reindeer of them all!' He leaned in and whispered. 'Shh, though. Don't tell the others. Dasher and Dancer and Donner and Blitzen will not be happy!'

He got to his feet and stood, straightening out his belly and turning to Nell, motioning that she was to join in.

He noticed the fear in her eyes. Did she not like to sing? Or was she just embarrassed?

'A one, two, three...'

They began to sing, and instantly he flinched and turned, shocked at the sounds coming out of Nell's mouth.

She couldn't sing!

He wanted to laugh so hard, but he didn't want to ruin the song for Peyton. So he turned away from his Little Elf and tried to ignore the caterwauling behind him as she bravely tried to hit the notes with him and continued on with the song.

He made eye contact with Peyton, who was

chuckling, and made a *Have you heard this?* motion with his thumb at Nell behind him.

He boomed out the lyrics and noticed the smiles on all the other children's faces as they listened and laughed at Nell, whose face was going redder and redder. But he had to give her points. No matter how awful she sounded, she bravely ploughed on, singing the song for Peyton. As they reached the final line Nell's voice cracked and she made a weird choking sound. He couldn't help it. He laughed. Laughed so hard his belly began to jiggle. And then all the children joined in.

Yet when he looked at Nell, expecting her to be embarrassed or to run away, cheeks burning, he found that she was laughing too, barely able to breathe, clearly enjoying her own inability to sing and how awful she sounded, but not caring because it had made Peyton and all the other kids on the post-surgical ward laugh.

They'd brought joy and song and laughter to a ward that didn't often have any.

The kids all began to clap, and one, the little boy in the far bed, cheered and whooped.

Seth reached into his sack and pulled out a wrapped gift for Peyton. 'Merry Christmas,' he said, leaning in so she'd hear him. 'I shall hope and pray that one day your wishes come true.'

'Thank you, Santa.'

He gave her a wave and then, with his Little Elf, went to the next ward.

Afterwards, Nell and Seth made it back to the staff room at the end of a long afternoon. She'd not realised how exhausting it would be, and she had new-found respect for Santa's grotto staff all over the globe.

She pulled off her red velvet hat and her jingling boots and flopped down on the sofa. Behind her, Seth peeled off the Santa jacket and his fake belly and beard and sat opposite her in just Santa's trousers and a fitted white tee. He had muscular arms that spoke of time spent in the gym. She wanted to look away, but to be honest she was kind of surprised.

Seth as Santa had shown her an entirely different side to the man she'd thought she knew, and now she wondered if there was more to him than she'd initially suspected. For her, the battle lines had come down, at least for a short while, and she wanted to know more about this man before the ceasefire ended.

'We did a good thing today,' she said.

He nodded and ran his hands through his thick dark hair. 'I hope so. Not sure my ears will recover from that voice of yours...but we're in a hospital. I can get ENT to take a look before I go home. Make sure no real damage has been done.'

He grabbed a biscuit off a plate and bit into it.

Nell smiled. 'Yeah. I should have told you before that I can't sing.'

'Can't sing? It sounded like there was something mortally wrong with your vocal cords. Cats for miles around were wondering why their queen was calling them. I wouldn't be surprised if when we leave the hospital it's surrounded by moggies.'

She laughed. 'I know! But I wasn't going to stop. Peyton wanted us to create magic today, and we couldn't, so instead she asked for a song. I would have given that girl whatever was in my power to make her happy.'

He nodded sagely. 'Some of those kids have it tough. That old saying, *Well, at least you have your health…* They don't even have that.'

No. Nell knew all about kids who didn't have their health.

Lucas's face flashed into her mind. How he'd looked lying there in that hospital bed, all pale. It had been better when he was sleeping, because then he hadn't felt unwell. He'd been in a land of dreams.

That was how she'd dealt with his coma. She'd told herself he was just sleeping. She would carry the pain, the hurt and the grief, whilst Blake sat beside her in a chair, sighing and playing some stupid game on his phone to pass the time.

Thankfully he'd only come on occasion. He'd told her that there was no point in them both sitting there, day after day, as Lucas had no idea they were there. But the nurses had told her that maybe he could hear their voices, and so she would sit and read Lucas stories, hoping that her voice would somehow bring him back to them after his aneurysm.

Before he'd got sick, Lucas would often wake in the middle of the night, come and tell her his dreams. She would have given anything for him to do that back then.

Only he'd never woken up. He'd just faded away. Slowly. Day by day. And there'd been nothing she could do to prevent it.

So Nell knew how those parents felt as they sat beside their children's beds, hoping and praying that they'd get better and come home. And she knew how scared those kids were, too. Not truly understanding what was going on, but trusting the adults and the doctors and nurses to make them better.

Seth sat forward suddenly, arms resting on his knees, looking intrigued. 'Where did you go just then?' he asked in a soft voice.

Nell met his gaze. Should she tell him? Did he need to know? Did she need to share Lucas with him? Maybe. Perhaps he might look at her in a kinder, more compassionate light.

'I was thinking about my son.'

A pause. A raised eyebrow as he looked at her differently.

'You never mentioned you had a son.'

She smiled grimly. 'I don't have him. Not any more.'

Seth's eyes darkened as he frowned. 'I'm sorry.' He sounded it too. 'You don't have to tell me anything if you don't want to.'

Nell appreciated that respect. This was her choice. He wasn't demanding information from her, and yet somehow that made her want to give it.

'His name was Lucas. He died three years ago. The night you and I met, when my car was in the ditch, was the third anniversary of his death. I was returning home from visiting his grave. I couldn't miss it. Not even for bad weather.'

Seth managed to look completely and utterly ashamed. He looked down at the floor. 'And I was awful to you... About being out in that weather. I'm sorry. I should have realised you'd have a good reason.'

'You weren't to know.'

'No. But I could have been kinder. You were having a difficult day already. Then your car ended up in a ditch. I ought to have been more…considerate.'

He had the decency to look shamefaced.

She smiled. 'Yes. You should have been.'

'I'm sorry. I mean it.'

Nell was kind of enjoying this version of Dr Seth James. She'd seen a completely different side to him when they were with the children. He'd been kind and funny and generous. Warm! And, although she'd been dreading having to be his elf for the day, it had actually been fun. And now, seeing this tender side of him… She was beginning to realise that she had misjudged him completely. That the Seth she'd met on that winter's night in a blizzard was not the real Seth.

'It's okay,' she said.

'No. It's not. And I guess if we're being honest with one another perhaps I ought to tell you why I wasn't in the best of moods when we met, either.'

'Go on.' She was intrigued. Anything to explain that night…

'That bend where your car went into the ditch…'

She nodded.

'It was the exact spot in which my girlfriend

was killed, when she skidded on black ice and careered into a tree at speed. I survived. As did our son, Olly. But Dana succumbed to her injuries.'

'Dana!'

Of course! Nell remembered hearing about her accident! Dana had once been a friend. They'd met at secondary school, never in any of the same classes, but often in the school plays. They'd both liked to act, and one year had both auditioned for the role of fairy god-mother in the pantomime. They'd had a bit of a rivalry. Friendly and fun. Joking and winding each other up. They had known one another. A little anyway.

Nell had been away in Austria with Blake when the accident had happened. She'd found out about Dana's death when she'd returned and her obituary had been in the local news-paper.

'You knew her?'

Nell nodded. 'Once upon a time. Many years ago. At school. I remembered reading that she'd died… I didn't know she was your girlfriend.'

Seth looked down. 'So, finding you in that spot, in a car, in a ditch, in the middle of a blizzard that everyone had been advised not to drive in… It shook me. I'm not ashamed to admit it.'

'I get that. And I'm sorry. How is Olly coping?' The boy… The boy who had been standing in her bedroom that morning when she'd woken at Elmbridge Manor. Standing there holding that teddy…

'He's doing okay. As well as can be expected. He asks questions about his mum sometimes, and I guess he'll find out the truth one day.'

'The truth? Of the accident?'

'The fact that if it wasn't for me wanting to have a drink at a Christmas party she'd still be here today.'

To give her credit, Nell tried to say it wasn't his fault.

'You can't blame yourself.'

'Can't I?' He sat back on the couch and let out a long, low breath. 'I wanted a drink. A *drink*, for crying out loud! And because of that she offered to fetch me and bring me home afterwards. With Olly in the car! If I hadn't had a drink…if I'd driven myself…then she'd still be here and Olly would have his mother.'

'Maybe, but no one could blame you for wanting a drink at Christmas. At a party. She did a nice thing, offering to pick you up. And who's to say that *you* wouldn't have skidded on that same patch of ice as *you* drove home? Then Olly wouldn't have his dad.'

'Better that than not having his mum…'

'You can't think that. What happened, happened. No amount of guilt or regret will change the past. But you can be the one to give him all his future happiness. The love of a father who will no doubt be his bedrock and his go-to guy.'

'You're sweet to be so kind. Especially after how I've spoken to you.'

She laughed gently. 'We have had our moments.'

He sat forward again and held out his hand. 'Ceasefire?'

He didn't want to be on her case any more. Didn't want to tease her or rile her or any of those things. They'd both been through loss. They'd both lost someone special. Her, a son. Him, the mother of his child. There was no need for them to be at war any more. They ought to be united in their shared pain.

'Ceasefire.' She leaned forward and shook his hand. 'The official peace treaty begins now.'

He let her hand go, trying not to think too hard about what it had felt like to touch her. Had it been something magical? Something warmly intriguing? Or was it just relief that they had made a pact to be nicer to one another?

Dismissing it as nothing more than that, he smiled and stood up. 'Well, time to get changed. I don't want to drive home like this.'

She looked down at her own outfit. 'No.'

'And don't forget to take off all of that.'

He pointed at his own face, indicating the make-up on her cheeks. The big circles. The freckles. They were cute, though. Made her look impish. Like a pixie. A beautiful pixie.

'I won't.' She stood and met his gaze for a moment. 'It's nice to finally meet you, at last, Dr Seth James.'

He nodded and smiled. 'Likewise, Nell Bryant. Likewise.'

CHAPTER SIX

IT BECAME HARD not to notice Seth after that. Now, when they had to pass each other on the wards or see each other across the room, instead of feeling a rising irritation and waiting to defend herself from his smarmy comments, Nell found herself smiling at him, or nodding, or saying hello and asking how he was doing.

And it was having a strange effect.

It was odd how sharing the story of losing Lucas had opened up a whole other avenue of friendship between them. She liked this new intimacy they shared. Liked it that they now understood one another and where they were coming from.

One lunchtime, just as she was heading off the ward to get something to eat, Seth bumped into her and asked if he could join her for lunch.

'I'm starving. Haven't eaten all morning.'

'Sure,' she answered.

The hospital cafeteria was busy and there weren't many hot food options left, but Nell settled on a chicken pie with some mashed potatoes and veggies, and Seth had fish and chips with mushy peas. There was a table by the window, overlooking the memorial park, so they sat there.

'How's Olly?' she asked.

'Good. He's been given a role in his school's Christmas play and the first show is tonight. He's nervous, even though he's only got a small bit to do.'

'What's the play?'

'Something called *The King's Christmas Cherries*.' He laughed at her expression. 'No, I've never heard of it, either.'

'What part has he got?'

'He plays a knight. Only one line. He has to bow before the King and say, *"Your Majesty! I bring you Sir Cleges!"*'

'Has he been practising?'

'Are you kidding? I've heard every iteration of that sentence for the last week or two. It's driving me mad.'

'But you won't feel mad when you hear him say it in the play. You'll be proud.' She pointed her fork at him and smiled. She would have loved to see Lucas in a school play, but he'd

been sick. But she would never get that chance
now. 'A proud papa.'

He nodded, obviously thinking hard. 'Yeah.
Would you want to come with me? Go and
watch it together?'

What?

Her heart suddenly pounded in her chest at
his suggestion.

Isn't that... I don't know...a little odd?

'I barely know him.'

Seth looked embarrassed. 'Of course! Sorry.
I don't know what made me ask. It's just...
These things, you know? Things that both parents usually go to. I hate going on my own. It
just makes me think that Dana should be there,
too. Reminds me that she's not there.'

Without thinking, Nell reached across the
table and squeezed his hand. Just briefly. 'She
would have loved it. Seeing her son in a school
play like she used to be...'

He frowned, looking up at her. 'How do you
know she liked to act?'

'I told you—I knew her at school. We usually went after the same parts in the school
plays and pantomimes. She loved acting. I
think she'd love the fact that her son is doing
the same thing even more.'

Seth smiled sadly and she made a sudden
decision.

'You know what? For Dana's sake I will go. I'd love to go and see *The King's Christmas Cherries* with you.'

'What made me say I'd go?'

The question kept going around and around in her brain that afternoon at work. Seth had left for home. He'd worked the early morning shift and stayed until two in the afternoon, and now he had left after giving her a time to meet.

Suddenly their ceasefire, their friendship, seemed to be heading in another direction, and she was worrying that she was getting too close.

As she helped place an IV in a young patient who was going to be having surgery that evening for the removal of a foreign object—she had a coin stuck in the distal end of her oesophagus—she saw her friend Beth looking at her.

'What's up? I've never seen you frown so much.'

'Oh, nothing.' She didn't want to talk about it in front of their patient.

'No, come on. Something's bothering you!'

'Mummy always says a problem shared is a problem halved,' said the patient.

'Mummy's right,' insisted Beth. She slipped

her arm into Nell's and pulled her away from the bedside. 'Come on—spill.'

Nell sighed. 'I've agreed to go somewhere with someone and I'm not sure I should have.'

'Well, that's a little vague... Is the someone a guy?'

She nodded, biting her lip.

'Whoa! Okay. You've not been on a date since Blake.'

'It's not a date! I've just agreed to accompany him to something, that's all.'

'Honey, that's a date.'

'What am I going to do?'

'You could cancel if you're uncomfortable. Say something's come up. Do you like him?'

A few days ago she would have said no. But since he'd been Santa and she his elf, and since that moment of sharing their painful pasts in the staff room, things had changed. She'd seen another side to him, and if she were truly being honest then, yes, she liked him.

It must have shown on her face, because Beth's eyebrows rose in surprise. 'Okay. Well, I guess the question is...do you feel ready to date again?'

'I'm not sure he sees it as a date. He didn't ask me out, exactly. Well, he did, and I said no, and then I changed my mind and offered to go with him.'

'Wow. The romance!'

Nell smiled ruefully. 'It's just as friends, I think.'

'You need to be sure.'

'I only ask because if things don't work out and get awkward, you're going to have to continue to work in the same place, and that can get uncomfortable.'

Nell nodded. But she'd already dealt with the uncomfortable with Seth, and if they ended up back there again she'd deal with it. Somehow. But he wouldn't be interested in her in *that* way. Would he? He had a son to think about, and she... Well, she didn't. And she wasn't looking to be anyone's stepmother, or anything. She wouldn't be able to handle that.

'I'm just going to support him on what could be a difficult thing. That's all.'

'He needs a bit of hand-holding? I see... Okay. Well, then you need to make it clear what you're offering here. Friendship. Nothing more.'

But again something must have shown on her face, because Beth tilted her head, smiled and leaned in closer.

'Unless...you *do* want something more with him?'

Nell blushed. She'd be lying if she said she hadn't thought briefly about what it might be like to be kissed by Seth. He was dark and brooding. The lord of the manor, with a tragic back story of heartbreak and looks to kill for. He was strong and broad-shouldered. He looked the kind of guy who would be able to protect you for life.

And she knew he loved deeply. He had been devoted to his girlfriend, Dana. Had given her the kind of love that Nell could only dream of.

Blake had never been demonstrative. Never been one for public displays of affection. She had yearned sometimes for him to hold her hand or tell her he loved her in public. But their relationship had never been overly physical. It was something that had plagued her for years, but she'd accepted it because back then she had loved Blake and wanted to accept him for the way he was. The way he showed love. It would be enough, she'd kept telling herself.

But then Lucas had died and the wedge, the gap between her and her husband, had widened. His inability to show emotion, or anything of what he was feeling, had been the final nail in the coffin of their marriage, and she couldn't remember the last time she'd been held. The last time she'd been kissed.

She yearned for human touch.

To be cherished and loved for who she was. Made to feel important to someone. As if she was the only one who mattered. The only girl in the world.

So, yes, she did want something more.

The question was…did she want all that from Seth?

And, more importantly, was he even capable of giving it?

It had felt strange, asking Nell to join him at his son's school to watch him in a play. It wasn't even as if Olly had a big part! It was just one line…it would be over in a jiffy.

But the idea of sitting in the audience alone, with all the other proud parents…

Dana would have loved it! She'd have been excited, telling Olly how proud they were, and that he was going to be amazing and not to be nervous. She would have tried to get a front row seat and recorded it on her phone, or taken pictures, and she would have cheered the loudest at the end, standing to clap and maybe even give a wolf whistle or two when the cast came on stage to take a bow.

He knew this because that was what she had done when Olly had been an angel in his first ever Christmas play at nursery.

Since Dana's death, Seth had endured these torturous events for Olly's sake only. Sitting at the back of the auditorium, trying not to notice all the couples, all the proud mums and dads sitting together, and trying in vain not to hate them because they had what he and Olly didn't. And when the play was over, he'd collect Olly and whisk him home again. Telling him that he was proud. That Olly had done well.

Why had he invited Nell? Just so that he wouldn't be there alone again? So that Olly had two people applauding him? Who would Olly think she was? He'd not thought that through, and that bothered him—that he'd asked her so impulsively. She didn't really want to go. She'd said no, originally. Well, kind of…

'I barely know him.'

She was right. They'd met once. When she'd been sleeping over at the Manor. And if he were to turn up at his son's school with her in tow what would Olly think? She was just a friend. A work colleague he'd helped out once. But would his son understand that?

He'd dropped his son off and left him with the teachers, so that he could get dressed in his knight's outfit, and now Seth was standing outside the school, waiting for Nell to arrive. He'd told her a time to meet him.

He glanced at his watch. She should have been here ten minutes ago.

Had she changed her mind? Did she think the invitation was weird and regret accepting it? She'd taken pity on him, that was all. It had been an impulse offer to come.

Seth managed a polite smile at the one or two parents he knew, whom he saw on drop-offs and pick-ups. He watched the couples, walking in excitedly. One or two were arm in arm.

The Painters, as always, held hands. They had twins. They said the months of sleepless nights had helped bring them closer together. That as the twins babbled in their own secret language that they didn't understand it made them talk to one another more. Brought them closer.

Seth envied them that. He'd always thought he'd grow old with Dana. Marry her.

He'd never understood her reasons for not wanting to marry. She'd said her parents should never have married. That they spent all their time arguing. Told him how she constantly had to hear how her mother could not afford to move out so had to stay with a man she hated.

It had had an effect on Dana. She'd remained steadfastly independent in their relationship. Kept her own bank account. Worked at her own career and always been wary of the title that would come if she married the Lord of Elmbridge Manor. She'd said that anyone who married into that kind of rich history would be taking a lot onto their shoulders, and he'd agreed, but he'd thought they could do it.

They'd been happy, hadn't they? But though he'd asked Dana to marry him more than once, she'd kept saying no.

It had hurt. But he had loved her and respected her wishes. Even if he'd felt that she was never truly his. That somehow she always had one foot out through the door, ready to bolt.

He checked his watch again. Five more minutes and then he'd go in. He was probably being a fool to expect her to turn up. Olly was nothing to do with her. She wouldn't feel any pride in watching him perform. She'd be polite, smile and clap, maybe, but that was it.

No. He'd asked her here for himself. And if she didn't show up wouldn't work be awkward? Especially since they'd called a ceasefire after their initial meeting?

And then suddenly he saw her. Or rather, heard her first. There was the sound of running footsteps, heavy breathing, and then there she was, dark hair streaming behind her as she ran up to him, smiling, laughing, panting.

'Oh, thank God! I thought I'd be too late!'

'It's fine. Why are you running?'

'My car. I swear it's more trouble than it's worth.'

'What happened?'

'It conked out on me halfway here. Steam rising from under the bonnet… I'm wondering if the accident cracked something and it's finally given up the ghost? Anyway, I've had to abandon it a few streets away.'

He smiled. 'You're going to get your money's worth out of your breakdown membership.'

'Well, they've had enough money out of me over the years.' She looked past him. 'Where's Olly?'

'Getting into his costume. Ready to go in?' She nodded.

'Thanks for this. I do appreciate it.'

Her eyes met his and he saw them soften. 'You're welcome.'

If she had been Dana he would have taken her hand, kissed her cheek, and they'd have walked in together. But he couldn't kiss Nell or take her hand, so he awkwardly put his hands into his jeans pockets and said, 'This way, I think. Follow the crowd.'

He showed his parent pass to the teaching assistant who was manning the door and then they walked down a school corridor that smelt of paint and clay and books. They were herded, like sheep, into the school hall.

Up at the front was a raised stage, with red

curtains covering its entirety, and the rest of the room was filled with milling parents, looking for the last good seats.

Seth scanned the rows, looking for two seats together. He and Nell were the last two people in, it seemed, and he wasn't sure where they would sit—until he saw the headmistress, Mrs Janlin, trying to get his attention and pointing to a couple of seats two rows back from the front, hidden by a sea of heads.

'Thanks,' he said, as they passed the headmistress, and then he stood back to let Nell go first.

Sitting down, he saw they had a good view of the stage.

Nell leaned in. 'I did some research and I think this play is based on a story involving King Arthur.'

'Really?'

He was impressed that she'd done any research at all. Olly wasn't her kid, so for her to show that kind of interest… He was kind of pleased.

As the lights were lowered and some medieval-sounding music began to play, the hubbub of the crowd decreased, spotlights rose on the stage and the curtains pulled back to reveal a king sitting on his throne, examining a bowl of grapes and frowning.

'These grapes taste of nothing!' said the boy dressed as the King, loudly. 'I wish I had some fruit that tasted delicious!'

The play was more interesting and a lot funnier than Seth had thought it might be. At times, the audience roared with laughter. And they clapped and cheered when a nervous young girl performed a solo vocal, tremoring with fear to begin with, but eventually gaining confidence and letting her voice soar like an angel.

They smiled quietly when some of the children stumbled or fumbled through their lines. And then suddenly Olly was there, striding on stage in his knight's uniform and standing before the King.

He gave an exaggerated bow and announced in a loud voice, 'Your Majesty! I bring you Sir Cleges!'

Seth couldn't help it. He beamed with pride. It was only one line. Olly didn't have a major part. But his son had acted the part of a noble knight perfectly. And as the tattily dressed Sir Cleges entered, stage right, Olly stood behind the King's throne, relieved that his part had gone without a hitch. He sought out his dad's face in the crowd and gave him a little wave.

Seth waved back.

'He did brilliantly!' whispered Nell.

'He did.'

Was that a tear he could feel in his eye? A tear of pride? Because he'd never felt so proud as he did in that moment, and he hoped that if Dana was somehow able to see her son, she would feel proud, too.

Seth stared at his son until he left the stage, and then he watched the rest of the play, laughing with the audience when Sir Cleges chased the knights with his stick and all devolved into chaos on stage as the kids went crazy.

The King's Christmas Cherries turned out to be an amazing play, and when it was over the entire audience stood and gave the kids a standing ovation.

Seth whistled loudly, and beside him Nell clapped heartily.

'That was so good!' she yelled, so that he could hear.

She was right. It had been more than good. It had been amazing. And he couldn't have been more proud of his son than he was in that moment.

Afterwards, Mrs Janlin gave a few announcements and handed out some award certificates. Olly was called up to receive a certificate for 'Asking the Most Awkward Questions in Assembly'.

Seth felt there must be a story or two behind that certificate, and he couldn't wait to hear what it was.

As they stood outside, waiting for Olly to appear, he took the moment to thank Nell again for coming. 'I really appreciate it,' he told her.

'Hey, I had a great time! Back when I was Olly's age school plays were awkward, embarrassing affairs, with difficult silences when everyone forgot their lines. Kids today seem much better at it than we were.'

He laughed. 'I think you're right. Olly did so well… I feel I ought to treat him. Fancy a bite to eat? Or do you have to go? I don't want to take up all your free time if you have somewhere else to be.'

He watched her think about it for a moment. 'No, I don't have anywhere to be. If that's okay with you and Olly?'

'I'm sure he won't mind.'

At that moment, Olly came barrelling out of school, grinning, his face lit up, holding on to his certificate.

'Look, Dad, look!'

'I saw! Congratulations!' Seth read the certificate that had been waved in his face, then passed it to Nell to look at. 'You remember Nell? You met her at home the other day?'

Olly peered up at her. 'You had a sleepover at our house.'

'Er...that's right,' said Nell, awkwardly.

'I thought we could grab a bite to eat, Olls. Is it okay if Nell comes, too?'

'Sure.'

Seth smiled at Nell, and they began to head out of the car park.

Olly was a bundle of energy, clearly high on his stage debut and being awarded a certificate. He held on to his dad's hand, but he was so bouncy and so full of adrenaline Nell felt exhausted just watching him.

She'd forgotten how vital and high-octane some little boys could be. Lucas had been the same when he'd got excited. She was dismayed at how difficult she was finding it, being in his company. Olly was so full of energy, so full of life. It simply reminded her of what she'd lost.

Seth took them to a pizza restaurant, where Olly ordered cheese and tomato. Seth ordered a meat feast, and Nell asked for a small vegetarian pizza with extra mushrooms and jalapenos.

She was relieved when Olly disappeared to play in the soft play area whilst they waited for their food to arrive.

'You okay?' Seth asked.

She nodded, forcing a smile. 'Yes. You?'

'I am. I spent a long time dreading tonight and you made it easier.'

'Oh, I'm sure it was nothing to do with me. Olly is the star of the night.'

'Well, that too. And now I'll never have to hear about Sir Cleges again!'

'Bonus.' She laughed, twirling the straw in her glass of water.

'I know this must be hard for you… Christmas is a time for families. Especially those with young children. You should be the one watching your son in a play, and yet there you were with me, watching mine. That was more than generous. That was brave and kind and I won't ever forget it.'

Nell wasn't used to a man saying nice things about her in public. She wasn't used to sitting in a restaurant across from a man and having him stare into her eyes and tell her how much he appreciated her.

It was weird.

It was strange.

But most of all it was wonderful, and delicious, and she craved more. But they were just friends, right? She'd done this as a favour to him. It hadn't been a date. This wasn't a romance. And yet it didn't stop her from blushing and thinking what it might be like if it were…

What kind of romantic partner was Dr Seth James, Lord Elmbridge? She'd seen and experienced his sarcastic side. The smart-aleck

side. She'd seen the sort of doctor he was—
kind and warm. She'd seen him as Santa Claus
and knew he could be funny and generous and
thoughtful. Clearly, he was a complex man.

But could he love?

He'd been through loss, just as she had.
She'd lost a son and a marriage and it had left
her wary of ever being with someone again.
Her marriage had taught her a lot about what
she didn't want from a relationship. And what
she did want. If she were ever brave enough
to dip her toe in the dating waters ever again
she'd want to be loved openly. By someone
who was physical in their love. Who believed
in the power of hugs and cuddles and kisses.
Who was openly demonstrative. Someone she
could hold at night and fall asleep in his arms
feeling that she was adored and valued and
cherished.

What did Seth want? After Dana, did he
ever feel he could date again?

'What are you thinking?' he asked.

Blushing, she laughed. 'Oh…deep thoughts.'

'Want to share?'

'Here? In a pizza restaurant?'

'Why not?'

She stared at him, wondering if she was
brave enough to ask. Feeling her cheeks burn.

'Okay… I was wondering if you ever saw yourself dating someone again.'

Seth let out a short laugh of surprise and leaned away from her in his chair. 'Not what I was expecting!'

She saw him check to see where Olly was.

'Maybe. One day. But at this point I'd be pretty surprised if I did. That person would have to be amazing enough to thaw my ice-hardened heart and warm it up enough to make me go through all that palaver again.' He stared hard at her. 'What about you?'

'Me? Oh, I don't know… I think Blake might have ruined me for a while.'

'Your husband?'

She nodded. 'It was just so awful and so difficult at the end… The person who is meant to love you shouldn't treat you like that, you know? And if someone who is meant to love you can treat you so badly…? Well, I've heard enough shocking dating stories from my friends at work that I'm not sure I want to enter that world again. Maybe one day I'll be brave enough, but not right now.'

'What made you think of that now?'

She sipped her water. 'Tonight. Seeing all those happy families at the school. Realising I'm not one of them any more. I felt lonely. I may not have Lucas, but I'm still a mother. A mother without a child. And it's Christmas. A time for families. I really feel it at this time of year.'

'I get that. I don't feel like I'm one of them, either.'

'You don't?'

'Absolutely not. Olly should have his mum here with us. Getting excited. Watching his shows. Going to parents' evenings. Every time I go to one of those things on my own I'm harshly reminded that I shouldn't be. On my own, that is.'

'Don't we make a pitiful pair?' she said ruefully.

At that moment a server arrived, carrying their pizzas.

Seth called out to Olly, and when the young boy came to the table made his son clean his hands, using an antibacterial wipe from a small sachet. 'Okay, now you can eat.'

Nell watched as Olly smeared his pizza with extra ketchup and smiled. Lucas had liked ketchup, too.

It felt odd to be sitting there with Seth and his son. She was a part of this small group, yes, but she didn't belong. Not really. She was an outsider, allowed in by Seth's grace. Nothing more.

Her pizza was perfect. Oozing with melted

cheese and soft mushrooms, with a kick from the jalapenos and peppers. It hit the spot. And although she felt on edge, she had to admit it was much better than being at home in her flat alone, searching the channels on the TV to find something that took her fancy.

Christmas was always difficult without Lucas. Far too quiet. Far too tidy. She'd put up some decorations and a tree, but it was something that she did out of duty now. Before, she would get Lucas to help her decorate. Lifting him up to place the star or the angel on the top of the tree. Getting him to put his stocking over the end of his bedpost. Her stocking hung alone now on the mantel. A glaring reminder of her solitude.

Her mum and dad always suggested that she go to them at Christmas. But with her work commitments she'd have to take too much time off from work. And besides, she'd spent enough Christmases with them and really didn't want any more.

Not with Mum getting angry with Dad for having one too many extra drinks as he cooked dinner, or Dad getting leery and making one too many jokes at Mum's expense, so that by the time Christmas Day turned into Christmas Night there'd be an atmosphere that could be cut with a knife, punctuated only by her father's deep, resonant snores from the couch. Her mum only ever wanted her there as a buffer. So she'd have someone to moan to.

Nell didn't want that any more. She wanted to sit and remember the good times. Reflect and quietly toast her son as she sat down to Christmas dinner.

'Are you my dad's girlfriend?' Olly suddenly asked out of nowhere, with smudges of ketchup around his mouth.

Nell flushed and glanced with embarrassment at Seth.

'No, she is not,' said Seth, firmly and sternly to his son. 'I told you. She's a girl who happens to be a friend.'

'I know. But Jacob said that when *his* daddy has a lady sleeping over at their house, it's because she's his girlfriend.'

Nell's cheeks felt as hot as the surface of the sun. 'That's different,' she managed. 'The reason I was at your house was because my car had broken down in the snow storm and your dad offered me a place to stay. Otherwise I would have frozen in my car.'

Olly shrugged. 'Okay.'

Nell glanced again at Seth, glad she'd cleared that up. It had been awkward... Olly suggesting she was his dad's girlfriend.

'But Daddy will have a girlfriend one day, won't he?' Olly went on. 'Like Jacob's daddy?'

Nell swallowed hard and tried to redirect the conversation. 'Who's Jacob?' she asked.

'A boy in his class,' said Seth darkly.

'He has a mummy…but sometimes his daddy has a girlfriend, too.'

Nell looked to Seth for clarification.

'Jacob's parents are divorced.'

'Oh. I see.'

'Jacob says one day he will have *two* mummies.'

'And how does he feel about that?'

'I think he's happy. He smiled when he said it,' said Olly. 'But I don't think it's fair that he should have two when I don't even have one.'

Nell stared at the little boy, feeling his pain. She waited for Seth to say something, but he seemed tongue-tied, so she spoke instead. 'You do have a mummy, though, Olly. She will always be your mummy. She may not be here, in person, but you are never without a mummy.'

'You think so?'

She nodded. 'Absolutely. She loved you. I know it. With all her heart.'

The way she still loved Lucas. He wasn't here, but that didn't mean the love was gone. Not one iota.

'Love carries on,' she told Olly. 'Even when

that person we love is no longer with us in person. It's still here,' she placed a hand over her own heart, 'and will stay with you for ever.'

Olly smiled and then took another bite of pizza.

Nell met Seth's gaze and he smiled and nodded at her, mouthing a silent *Thank you*.

The rest of the meal went on without any more difficult conversation. Seth asked his son what the 'awkward questions' were that he'd asked in assembly, and before they all knew it they were laughing and enjoying each other's company.

For a very brief moment—a millisecond of time—Nell forgot that she was alone. Forgot that she wasn't a part of this small family group. But when it was time to go home, and she realised that she would have to walk away from them and leave them, she remembered, and the harsh reality of life almost took her breath away.

'Well, thank you for tonight. I had a great time,' she said to Seth. 'It was nice to meet you properly, Olly.' She shook the little boy's hand. 'And you made an excellent knight.'

'Let us drive you home,' said Seth. 'Your car's broken down, remember?'

'You don't need to rescue me twice. I'll be all right.'

'On the contrary. At least let us drive you to your car and wait with you until the breakdown service arrives.'

She shook her head. 'No. You go home. Olly's tired. Look at him yawning. I'll see you at work.'

Seth glanced at his son, who looked almost asleep on his feet. He'd had a long day. 'If you're sure?'

'Absolutely. Go.'

'All right. Thanks for coming with me tonight. I appreciate it.'

Nell smiled at him. 'You're welcome.'

And then he surprised her by leaning in and dropping a kiss on her cheek.

Nell held her breath and closed her eyes, slowing down time, feeling the moment as if wanting to treasure it. To remember it. His lips against her cheek…the soft bristles of his dark beard tickling her skin. The scent of him… Aftershave. Soap and sandalwood. Something deeper. Earthier.

She wasn't used to public displays of affection. Blake had only ever kissed her once in public, and that had been on their wedding day, when the vicar had said, 'You may now kiss your bride.' And he'd even looked awkward doing that!

And then Seth was pulling away, with something like regret in his eyes, taking his son's hand and helping him get into the car and do his seatbelt.

She stood there, watching them, knowing she ought to walk away. But she couldn't.

There'd been something in Seth's gaze when he'd kissed her goodbye…

He closed his son's car door and walked around to the driver's side. 'One last chance?'

He meant for a lift, but she found herself wishing he meant so much more.

'I'm good. It's not far. You get Olly home to bed.'

'Okay. See you at work tomorrow.'

She smiled. 'Yes. Yes, you will. Bye.'

She raised her hand as he got into the vehicle and continued to stand there as he drove away, her eyes tracking every last moment that his vehicle was in sight. When he disappeared around the bend she felt all the tension in her body flow out, and she practically sagged as she headed in the direction of her own car.

Alone once again.

CHAPTER SEVEN

SETH HAD BEEN called to the paediatric assessment unit. A young boy had been sent up from A&E with a week-long history of sickness and diarrhoea. And now he was reporting bad stomach pains.

When he got to the boy's bedside, he saw Jaxon Hunter's vitals were all alarmingly low. He saw a pale boy, clearly under-weight, who was also looking a little jaundiced, lying listlessly in bed, his anxious parents at his bedside. He was hooked up to an IV of fluids to help rehydrate him, and had been given anti-nausea and painkilling medication.

In A&E they'd taken blood, performed scans and an X-ray, and now it was Seth's job to report on the results.

'Mr and Mrs Hunter? I'm Dr James and I'll be looking after Jaxon. Do you want to tell me about how his symptoms began?'

Jaxon's mother spoke. 'He came home from

school a week ago, complaining of a tummy ache. They'd had the school Christmas dinner that day, and the teacher said the kids had all had pudding and sweets, so we just thought he'd indulged too much.'

Seth nodded.

'He seemed to be a little better the next day, but by the time he came home after school he said his tummy ache was back and he felt sick. That night he spiked a fever and had diarrhoea, so we thought maybe a tummy bug. Norovirus is around at this time of year, isn't it? Is that what this is?'

'We don't think so. Was he urinating frequently?'

'I don't know. Normally, I guess…'

'We'll need to get a sample from him. They weren't able to get one in A&E, so when he wants to go, if you could get it in a bottle so we can test it?'

'What do you think it is?'

Seth sighed. 'Well, normally these kinds of symptoms *would* be associated with a tummy bug or winter virus, but the yellowing of his eyes and skin indicate an issue with the liver. There have been some cases of healthy children this year suddenly developing acute hepatitis-like symptoms, due to an adenovirus, and at this moment in time I'm veering towards that.'

'*Hepatitis?* Isn't that serious?' the mother asked in shock.

'It can be, but if I'm right this isn't hepatitis as we normally imagine it. The adenovirus creates hepatitis-*like* symptoms—liver inflammation—so right now we need to treat Jaxon's symptoms and perform a PCR test to confirm.'

The polymerase chain reaction test would detect genetic material from a certain virus.

'And then he'll be okay?' asked Jaxon's father.

'We need to confirm our suspicions first, and then work from there.'

He didn't want to tell the Hunters that on occasion some children required liver transplants because of this virus. Why worry them until they knew for sure? They had enough to worry about with their son being in hospital as it was. He would tell them when they needed to know. When the evidence pointed in that direction.

'We'll need some more blood from Jaxon. I've already put the request in, so someone will be along soon to do it.'

'I'm here.'

Seth turned at Nell's soft voice and smiled on seeing her at the end of the bed. He'd not heard her approach. He turned back to Jaxon.

'This is Nell and she's going to take another small sample of blood from you—is that okay?'

Jaxon nodded.

Nell approached and sat on a chair beside the bed. 'Hi, Jaxon. I know you're feeling poorly, but I need to take some more blood from you.'

'They took blood in A&E. Can't you use that?' asked Jaxon's mother.

'That was used to test for other markers. I need a fresh sample for the PCR test. How are you with needles, Jaxon?'

'Okay... They pinch.'

'They do. But only for a little while.'

'The nurse in A&E struggled to find a vein,' said Jaxon's father. 'We don't want him poked all over again.'

Nell turned to face them. 'I get that. Totally. They might have struggled due to Jaxon's dehydration, but he's been on fluids for a while now, so hopefully I'll have better luck.'

Seth admired the way she was handling the parents' concern. She really was good at her job.

Nell palpated both of Jaxon's arms, focusing mainly on his left antecubital fossa—the crook of the elbow. Then she tied the tourniquet around his upper arm, swabbed with an alcohol wipe, gave it a brief second to dry, then inserted the needle and got a sample right away.

Seth had been holding his breath, but now he let it go. 'This is why we call Nell to do this,' he said, and smiled. 'We'll have the sample checked ASAP, so we can get the results to you. In the meantime, if you have any questions, don't hesitate to get a nurse to find me.'

'Thank you, Doctor.'

Seth escorted Nell back to the nurses' station, where she stood labelling Jaxon's sample, ready to bag it up and send it off to Pathology.

'How's your car?' he asked.

'Poorly. At the garage having its head gasket fixed, or replaced, or whatever it is they're doing.'

He grimaced. 'Sounds expensive.'

'It's fine. Christmas is meant to be expensive, right?'

'Not in that way. How did you get to work?'

'Bus.'

'Ah…'

'I bet you've never had to catch a bus in your entire life, huh?'

He smiled. Caught out. 'No, I haven't.'

'How the other half live…' She smiled as she sealed the bag with the blood sample. 'I'll get this off to Path.'

'Thanks. Hey, what time do you finish today?'

'Five.'

'Perfect. Me too. Let me give you a lift home.'

'You don't have to do that.'

'You helped me last night, so now it's my turn. Honestly, I don't mind.'

'Don't you have to get back for Olly?'

'He's at a friend's house. Sleepover.'

'Oh. Well, if you're sure…?'

He nodded. He absolutely was.

It was snowing again. But not as hard as the blizzard that had originally caused them to meet. This snow was gentle. Fat flakes drifting down and disappearing into the already wet ground. It wouldn't settle. Not this time. The ground was already sodden from the melt of the last snowfall.

It was nice being in Seth's car. It was a different one from the one that had been pulling the trailer that night they'd first met. This was a saloon car, with cream leather seats, and it was warm and comfortable. Gentle Christmas music played from the speakers.

'Left or right?'

She pointed ahead at the traffic lights. 'Right where that car's turning—see?'

'Yep.'

She wasn't sure how to feel about Seth seeing

where she lived. He lived out in the sticks—in a manor, for crying out loud! She wasn't sure he was used to suburban life and all that it entailed. Her flat in a tower block was all she'd been able to afford after the divorce, when they'd sold their marital home. She didn't plan on staying there for ever. She was saving hard, and she kept her expenses to a minimum, as much as she could—which was why the car breaking down was a big deal.

She needed the car for work, but repairing it really was money down the drain. She had considered telling the garage to scrap the car and be done with it, but in the end she'd not been able to. The car was her lifeline. It got her away from the town when she needed to breathe clean, country air. It got her to Lucas's grave at Wilford Hill. It got her away from the stresses and strains of living near a city as big as Nottingham.

'Take this left…then there's an immediate turning into the car park for my place.'

She saw him glance out at the huge tower block as he pulled into a parking spot.

'This is it,' she said. She didn't feel embarrassed about where she lived. She'd made it a home and she had good neighbours who helped each other out. But she just knew he'd be comparing it with where he lived and the vast differences between them.

'Which floor are you on?'

'Twenty-first. Top floor. I get a great view of Clifton and the city. Especially on fireworks night.'

'Must be amazing.'

'On occasion. Want to come up and see?'

The invitation was out of her mouth before she could even think to censor her words, and then she felt her cheeks burn as she blushed. Of course he'd say no. He wouldn't want to come in. Wouldn't want to risk leaving his car here.

'Sure!'

Nell blinked, surprised, but then she smiled and alighted from the car, waiting for him to lock it, then headed towards the entry doors. She swiped her security key on the front door pad. It buzzed and let her in.

On the ground floor was a security office, where Paul was on duty as usual.

'Hey, Paul, how you doing?'

'Hey, Nell! I'm doing fine. Readying myself for the night.'

'Can you do me a favour? Keep an eye on the silver saloon in the car park? The one under the lamp.'

'Can do.' He saluted her as they walked past and she punched the button for the lift.

She'd never have thought that she'd be bringing Seth back here! As she waited for the lift she tried not to let nervousness bubble up inside her, but she couldn't help it! What would she do once they reached her flat? Talk to him? Make him a cuppa? Give him a tour? It wouldn't be much of one. It'd be over in less than a minute. A tour of Elmbridge Manor would take a good hour in comparison!

The lift doors pinged open and they stepped inside. She was suddenly acutely aware of the graffiti within it. Perhaps it would have been okay if it was artistic, but it was just people's names. Tags. Nothing more.

They rode the lift in silence, with Nell struggling for something to say. Just when she'd decided on a topic that might be safe, the lift doors pinged open and they were at the top. Her flat was directly opposite the lifts.

'This is it. Home,' she said, unnecessarily.

But she was still nervous. Because the last time she'd been with Seth on a social level he'd kissed her goodbye, and when she'd finally got home to her flat and sat down she'd replayed that kiss over and over again.

It had just been a kiss. Friendly. It had said *Thank you for joining me tonight*. Nothing more. That was what she kept telling herself. But she was struggling to admit to all that she had felt as Seth had leaned in to kiss her. The heart in her mouth moment, watching him come closer, as if in slow motion, the anticipation of the kiss...

She'd been hesitant.

Afraid.

Excited.

She'd wondered what it might be like to have a real kiss from Seth. To have a man like him be interested in her. To have him be attracted to her.

No doubt it would be a wild ride!

But was she only wondering about it because it felt like far too long that she'd been starved of affection? Lucas had given great cuddles, but he'd been her little boy, and although she cherished the memories of what his hugs had felt like, after his death she had yearned to be held by her husband.

Blake had let her down in more ways than one, though, and the slow decay of their marriage had been extremely lonely as they'd drifted further and further apart.

Nell still wanted that physical contact. To be held. To feel safe. To feel cherished and important. Could she get that from a man like Seth? Was he even interested in her in that way?

'Living room. Kitchen through there.' She walked a little further down the hallway. 'Bathroom.' There was a long pause before she decided to push open the other door. 'My room.'

She gave him a polite, embarrassed smile. The decor of her flat was nothing to write home about. It did not have the sumptuousness or decadence that Elmbridge Manor had. There were no chequerboard floors here. There was carpet and linoleum. No tapestries or wallhangings. Just a couple of pictures that she'd found in a local charity shop and liked. No sweeping staircases. Just a short, dark corridor, with a sad-looking Monstera plant in the corner.

'Looks great.'

She laughed. 'Now I *know* you're just being polite. This isn't what you're used to.'

'Sit down for a moment,' he said. 'I've something to show you.'

Intrigued, she led them back to the living room and sat down on the sofa. Alarmingly, Seth sat right next to her, his mobile phone in his hand as he began to thumb through his photo album. He got to the spot he wanted and passed her his phone.

'Keep swiping left.'

Nell frowned and looked at the first picture. It was of a small living space. Yes, it had French doors that led out to a small balcony overlooking the sea, but the living space itself was minimal. A wooden floor with a rug. A simple sofa and a chair. A bookcase. A television.

'What am I looking at?'

'My home in Devon. Where Olly and I were living before we came back to Elmbridge.'

She swiped left. There was a small galley kitchen. Only a tiny bit larger than her own. More modern than hers, but the space was practically the same. *Swipe.* A bedroom. A double bed, one small side table piled with books. A lamp. Some reading glasses. *Swipe.* A young boy's room. Single bed with a football team duvet. *Swipe.* A bathroom, with both a bath and a separate shower cabinet. Simple. White tiles. Potted plants hanging from a shelf.

'We live quite modestly. Elmbridge belongs to the public. We've always had an open house. The place is all about allowing the public access to a historic building. It's not just mine, though we do live there now. But that...' he nodded at his phone '...was where we used to call home.'

She passed the phone back. 'It is rather modest. Lovely, but modest.'

He smiled. 'It's hard to be comfortable amongst so much history.'

'How long are you planning to stay at Elm-bridge?'

'We're back for good. Granny isn't getting any younger, and it's time that Olly began to learn about where he came from and what his responsibilities will be when he gets older.'

'And your Devon home?'

'It will always be there if we need to go back, or just want to spend some time by the sea.'

She heard something in his voice. 'You're missing it?'

He nodded. 'I was free there. Not bound by dark memories. Here... I've got obligations.'

'Being Lord Elmbridge instead of Dr James?'

'You've got it in one.'

'But there must be a part of you glad to be back in your ancestral home?'

'Of course! Granny makes it easier, and it's good for Olly to know his great-grandmother.'

'What about your parents?'

His eyes darkened. 'They died when I was very young.'

'I'm sorry.'

'It was quick. Or so the doctors tell me. My father had a massive heart attack one day and my mother died a few years later. After that, Granny raised me.'

She reached for his hand tentatively. Squeezed

it in a show of support. Trying to say, *I'm here for you.*

Seth looked down at their hands, then away and over at the mantelpiece. At the pictures there.

'Is that your son?' He pulled his hand free and got up and walked away from her.

Nell felt her overture of affection had not been well received. Was Seth like Blake? Was she going to follow a pattern of falling for men who were uncomfortable with displays of concern or care?

'Yes. That's Lucas.'

The picture was her favourite one of him. He'd been outside in their back garden, building a snowman as the snow continued to fall. Lucas's nose and cheeks were bright red. He had snow crystals in his hair and it looked damp. He was in his coat and wellies and gloves and he looked so happy. She'd snapped his picture as he'd stood there, holding glovefuls of snow to add to their snowman. He'd turned. Looked at her. Grinned. *Snap.*

Afterwards, when it had been time to eat, time to go in and get warm, she'd made hot chocolate and they'd watched a Christmas movie. When they'd got up the next morning all that had been left of the snowman was a small mound of frozen snow, two broken twigs and a stubby carrot lying alongside them.

'He looks like you. He has your eyes,' Seth said.

That pleased her. That her son had taken after her, more than he had his father. Lucas had had blond hair, unlike her. But brown eyes like hers. He might have had his dad's mouth, and most definitely his dad's ears, but everything else was all her.

'Thanks.'

'You must miss him.'

She took a shuddering breath, determined not to cry. 'I do.'

Seth turned to look at her, obviously hearing the catch in her voice. 'I'm sorry. I didn't mean to make you feel sad.'

'You don't make me feel sad. Not having him here does that. All the time. I can mask it in most places, but here… I'm afraid you've caught me without my usual armour.'

He was looking at her strangely. Intensely. His gaze drifted over her features, his eyes searing into her soul.

'Tell me about him.'

'Lucas? He was the kindest boy. Generous in every way. He'd offer to give you his last sweet. He'd let you lick his ice cream. His laughter was the best sound ever…'

If she closed her eyes she could almost still hear it.

'And when he hugged you he would squeeze you so tightly…'

She could feel tears approaching. Normally she would fight to keep them back, but here, at home, sharing this moment with Seth, she wasn't sure if she should or not?

She sniffed and gave a nervous laugh, wiped her eyes. But Seth reached up to still her hand.

She stopped breathing. What was he going to do?

He looked into her eyes. Saw her soul. Her tears. Her pain. But it also seemed as if he could see something else worth pursuing. Because suddenly he was wiping underneath her eyes with his thumb. Catching her tears.

Her heart began to thud. She'd thought that maybe he was like Blake when he'd pulled his hand away from contact with her earlier, but maybe she'd been wrong? Maybe he'd felt something between them too? Maybe he'd been afraid?

But now his touch was gentle. Caring. Warm and soft.

Looking up into his dark gaze, she could feel herself getting lost. But she didn't want to assume anything was going to happen, so she kept her hands still, by her sides, desperately afraid to reach up and embrace him. What if she was reading the moment wrongly? If she was wrong, that would be embarrassing.

But she didn't think she was. Not with that look in his eyes. Not with the way he'd wiped away her tears. Not with the way he was now holding her face. Tenderly. Cradling her as if he couldn't quite believe he was standing this close and gazing into her eyes.

'There's something about you, Nell…' he said softly.

'Oh?' Her heart was hammering in her chest.

'I can't get you out of my mind.'

'Sorry about that,' she whispered, knowing she wasn't sorry at all.

'I wondered if…if it would be all right if…'

'If…?'

'If I could kiss you right now…'

She felt her eyes widen. Felt all the remaining breath leave her lungs. Her blood pressure was soaring, her pulse thundering, every nerve-ending and every cell in her body lighting up, as if on fire.

But she couldn't speak. Couldn't answer him. Fearing if she did try to speak her voice would squeak so high that maybe only dogs would hear it.

Instead, she gave the slightest of nods.

Yes. You can. Yes, you must. I want you to.

His gaze dropped to her mouth and then moved back up to her eyes, as if taking in every detail of her before he finally allowed himself to succumb to his desire to kiss her. He came closer. Closer still. Until they were millimetres apart.

She gazed deeply into his dark blue eyes, finally allowing her hands to rise up and rest upon his chest. He felt solid. All muscle. Just as she'd hoped he would be. And her touch seemed to make his breathing unsteady.

It was a heady moment.

His mouth was tantalisingly close to hers. 'You're sure? Because if I do this, I don't know if I'll be able to stop,' he whispered, arousing her instantly.

She nodded. 'Then please don't stop. I beg of you,' she whispered.

And that was enough to make his mouth claim hers.

Atoms split. Fireworks exploded. His brain went into absolute meltdown as his lips met hers. It had been a long time since he'd kissed a woman in this way. There'd been no one since Dana. Years of keeping himself walled off from everyone and not letting anyone get close. But the one thing he'd learned about putting up walls was that, yes, they kept everyone out, but they also kept you prisoner. He'd been in solitary confinement for too long and Nell was setting him free.

At last.

There was a moment of guilt. A moment in which he almost stopped. Stepped away. Told her that this was wrong. That he was sorry. Asked her if she could forgive him.

But that moment passed the second their lips met. Because kissing Nell felt so right and so good he couldn't imagine himself ever wanting to end this. His hunger for her simply grew. He knew he wanted more, but he couldn't presume she felt the same way—even if she had sunk against him and was now kissing him back with just as much fervour as he.

He paused briefly, to take a breath. Pulled back to stare into her eyes. Eyes that were dazed with lust and yearning. A look that almost felled him.

'Nell...'

'What?'

'You're sure?'

She nodded. 'Are you?'

It was as if she was searching his soul now. Looking for signs of regret. He knew she didn't want to do this unless he felt absolutely ready too, and he appreciated that so much. She must know there might be doubts because of Dana.

'Most definitely.'

He trailed his lips along her jaw, giving her featherlight kisses as he exposed her neck and ran his lips down it, feeling the heat of her, the rapid pulse in her carotid, the warmth of her skin. And her scent! Like flowers in a meadow. Her hair soft and silken in his fingers.

Somehow they moved to her bedroom, stumbling past furniture, against walls, not willing for a moment to let each other go. Against her bedroom door, he felt her reach for his belt, pulling it free and loose before she attacked his buttons. He kicked off his shoes. Felt her go for his zip.

It was a disrobing frenzy, with clothes strewn only God knew where, but they finally made it to the bed and he laid her down upon it, gently lowered himself onto her. Their tongues entwined. They both knew that this moment would happen, that...

We don't have protection.

The thought unloaded itself and he felt himself curse inwardly.

'What is it?' she breathed.

'I don't have a condom.'

He looked into her eyes with regret, saw it mirrored there.

'Me neither.'

His arousal was straining at the leash. He

wanted her. Badly. But he could not allow anything to happen in case it put either of them at risk. She must have seen the look of apology in his eyes, because she reached for his face and turned him towards her.

'Hey…' She smiled. 'There are other things we can do until we get one.'

Mmm… I like the way you're thinking!

'Say more,' he whispered.

She stroked his face, ran her fingers over his mouth. 'We have lips. And tongues. Hands. And fingers…' She bit her lip as she looked up at him with daring. 'What do you think we could achieve with any of those?'

'Let's find out,' he responded, smiling, and began to kiss her again.

CHAPTER EIGHT

SHE WOKE, NAKED, in Seth's arms. Totally satiated. Warm and cosy. She'd not slept so well for years, or felt so safe as if she did there and then.

She didn't want to move and spoil the moment. If she could have stayed there for ever, she would have. But she knew she had to go to work, and Seth probably did, too.

Turning her head ever so slightly, she tried to peer at the clock.

Eight-fifteen. She needed to be at work by nine o'clock and she hadn't showered yet. But to deliberately pull free from his embrace when she was the little spoon and Seth lay wrapped around her...

She was starving, too.

Last night had been...bliss. Heaven. Perfection. Okay, maybe not exactly perfection, but close to it. She would have loved to have felt the length of him inside her, but all the other things they'd got up to instead had been pretty terrific!

If this was Seth's foreplay what would the main event be like? She'd never known intimacy like it. Blake had been good at sex—when they'd actually engaged in it—but it had never felt like this!

With Blake, sex had been hurried, almost. As if he was embarrassed to be engaging in it and only scratching an itch he felt from time to time. She'd tried initiating it with him on occasion, only to be shot down and made to feel like a sex-crazed fool who could only think of one thing, when she wasn't like that at all.

All she'd ever wanted was the intimacy. The becoming one. The feeling that she mattered and that her desires would be sated when she felt them.

Last night Seth had been intent on making sure she was satisfied. He'd taken his time. Enjoying her pleasure as much as he'd enjoyed his own when she'd returned the favour. They'd discovered each other's bodies like explorers. Teasing. Tempting. Bringing each other to the heights until they'd finally fallen asleep with exhaustion.

It was no wonder she was hungry and didn't want to move.

Because she'd never felt like this before.

Ever.

Who'd have thought she'd be experiencing it with a man she'd really not been sure she even liked when she'd first met him?

He must have felt her shift, because he groaned slightly as he emerged from sleep and squeezed her against his body. 'Where are you going?' he asked, his voice husky with sleep.

Nell smiled happily. 'Believe you me, I don't want to be going anywhere—but it's a quarter past eight, and I don't know about you, but I need to be at work for nine.'

She felt him nuzzle into her hair. 'Urgh… Me too. Fancy playing hooky? We could call in sick.'

And now she felt other parts of his body waking up in response to being right next to her… But although his suggestion was deliciously tempting, she could not allow herself to let down her colleagues. They depended on her, and if she didn't show up it might mean a patient receiving a delay in treatment or surgery.

'That is *so* tempting…but we can't.' She allowed her hand to reach back and caress his hip and thigh.

'Careful…' he growled.

She grinned. 'Why? What are you going to do?'

'Hmm…'

Suddenly he had rolled her onto her back and was above her, smiling.

'So many things.' He kissed her, then pulled back again. 'But you're right. We have patients. Enjoying you will have to wait until later.'

He rolled over and let her go. Nell grabbed a robe and slipped into it.

'I'm going to grab a quick shower.'

Seth growled and pulled a pillow over his face. 'Aargh! Please don't make me think of you all soaped up in the shower.'

She chuckled. 'Okay… Unless you want to join me?'

He pulled the pillow off his face and stared at her. 'We'd never get to work on time.'

She shrugged. 'Five minutes late is better than not turning up at all.'

He threw off the covers and stalked towards her, totally naked.

'Let's make it ten.'

He took her hand and pulled her, laughing, into the bathroom.

Ward rounds were always Seth's favourite part of the day. He got to check in with all the patients and see how they were doing. Find out how they'd progressed overnight and often-times send them home, where they belonged.

This was even more important as Christmas crept ever closer.

His last patient of the day to check on was Amadi, the young boy who'd been brought over to England to have his twisted foot operated on. The surgery had been a huge success, and Amadi was on day three of recovery.

Seth examined his wounds and checked for sensation and capillary refill on Amadi's toes. It all looked great. 'We'll need to get you set up for some physio and some exercises you can do in the meantime. But if you keep going like this, Amadi, then I don't see why you can't go home next week.'

'Home' wasn't really home for Amadi. It was a room in a hotel being paid for by the charity that had brought him over from Africa. He would stay there with his aunt until he began weight-bearing and learning to walk properly.

'Thank you,' Amadi said.

'Hey, it was absolutely our pleasure to have you here and to help you. When you're up on your feet and able to do more stuff, we'll have to have a game of football. What do you say?'

'Cricket?'

Seth laughed. 'Okay. Sure! I'm not very good, but I'll give it a go. It's a deal.' He held out his hand and Amadi shook it.

Once ward rounds were over, Seth was headed back to the desk to make a phone call when he saw Nell pass by on her way to Pixie Ward.

He paused in what he was doing, just to watch her. She moved with such grace. He felt a smile creep across his face as he watched her—until he noticed one of the nurses watching him. He stopped smiling and put his head down, as if reading some paperwork, and then he picked up the phone.

Last night with Nell had been…out of this world!

They'd laughed, talked.

Played.

And, dear God, that woman could do things to him…

He'd thought it might feel odd. His first woman to be intimate with since Dana. And, yes, it had. It had felt strange, especially as he'd not been sure he could ever be with someone again. But Nell had got through all his defences so easily. She'd got under his skin from day one, to be fair, although he'd never thought it would end up like this.

But why shouldn't he try to find some fun? Some happiness? It wasn't as if they were getting into a serious relationship here. It was lust. He'd had a lot to deal with these last couple of years, so why not let the lid off the pressure cooker once in a while?

His gaze returned to her briefly as she disappeared through the doors to Pixie Ward, and all he could think of was the way she'd looked in the shower that morning. Dark hair streaming down her back, hands placed on the shower tiles as he'd helped make sure that every inch of her was soaped...

Seth tried to think pure thoughts. Work thoughts. To get himself back under control again. But it was proving difficult.

He and Nell had been able to spend last night together because Olly had had a sleepover at a friend's house. He'd have to be back at the Manor tonight for his son, but he didn't want to take Nell there to stay, because what if Olly crept into his room in the middle of the night?

He'd told Olly that he and Nell were friends. Nothing more. He didn't want to confuse or lie to his son. And he couldn't say, *I don't know what she is* and then have her in his bed every night. He needed to be his son's role model, and that meant teaching him how to treat people.

No. They'd have to find another way to be together.

Nell was sad. She'd been tasked with getting an IV into a newly admitted patient, but there'd been absolutely no veins to access—even with the vein finder—so the medical team had had to take the time to drill through the leg, just beneath the knee, and create an intraosseous infusion, giving them access to deliver medications, fluids or blood products directly into the marrow of a bone.

The team had given their tiny patient a local anaesthetic and Nell had tried to distract him with bubbles and teddy bears and puzzles, but it had been a difficult case, and seeing the child in such distress had really upset her.

On occasion, her job made her feel helpless. Impotent. As if she had no power to help. Most days her work went by without a blip, and she would go home feeling she had accomplished something. But the days when it all went wrong and she felt she'd done nothing left her feeling wasted. It was a sting that never went away. She would always remember those days, and she hated that it was easier for her to remember the failures than all of her successes.

A psychotherapist she'd sat with at lunch one day had told her that it was a natural thing. That if Nell were to be given ten sets of feedback and nine were good but one was bad, she would focus on the bad one the most. It was part of being human. Wanting to be liked and accepted. Because hundreds and thousands of years ago it had meant safety to be part of a group. Feeling disliked, feeling ostracised, played on your nerves because it made you feel alone.

She pondered that for a while and wondered if it was true. If it was still the most primitive part of the brain that controlled how people felt today? Or maybe it was nothing to do with evolution. Maybe it was what had happened to Lucas?

She'd felt helpless watching her son lie in his hospital bed. Her role had switched from being staff to being a patient's mother. Having to just stand by and wait whilst doctors made decisions on her son's behalf had been frustrating. Of course they'd tried to include her and Blake in their thinking, but really there'd been nothing they could do to help Lucas except make him comfortable before they turned off the machines that were keeping him breathing.

All her medical knowledge, all her years spent looking after other people's children, and she hadn't been able to help her own. That inability to take away his pain, his suffering... She felt the same way when she couldn't get IV access. When she couldn't draw blood from a patient. When she couldn't site a cannula.

It was a reminder that she wasn't perfect. That she couldn't solve all the ills facing children when they came into hospital. She wasn't a superhero. She was just a phlebotomist. She was human and fallible and sometimes she'd fail.

As she headed back to the desk to find out what her next job was, a linen cupboard door opened, and an arm reached out and pulled her inside.

Seth.

She smiled. Laughed a little.

'What are you doing?' she asked as he pushed her up against a rack of blankets and pillows.

'I have something for you.'

'You do? What is it?'

'This.' He bent forward to kiss her on the neck. 'And this.' His next kiss was by her ear. 'And this.' The final kiss was on her lips.

Then he gently tipped her chin upwards, so that her lips could meet his, and she allowed all the stresses of the past hour to fizzle away into nothing.

Kissing Seth was perfection. Kissing Seth took away all the worries and the concerns of the world and all she could think of was what he was doing to her in that moment.

Their morning shower had been an enlightening moment. She'd never shared a shower with another human being. She was used to standing under the hot spray alone and having a perfunctory wash. This morning she'd discovered how sexy shower gel could be. How it felt to have a man's hands soap her and wash her all over. She trembled at the memory.

'And this.' Seth lifted a condom into view.

She laughed quietly. 'Where did you get that?'

'Oh, you know…store cupboards in hospitals are amazing things.'

'You stole it? You naughty man.'

'"Stole" is a strong word. *Purchased* is a better one. I dropped a few coins in the donations tin at the genito-urinary clinic.'

Nell laughed. 'So it's ours? And we're free to do with it what we wish?'

'Absolutely.'

His dark eyes had a devilish glint in them that aroused her in an instant, and she couldn't believe she'd have to wait until much later before she could take advantage of that.

'Where should we meet? My place?' she asked.

'I'm not sure I can wait that long. The door behind us has a lock, you know…' He winked.

'You want us to have sex in a linen cupboard? On a children's ward?'

He groaned. 'Maybe not. I guess you're right. That would be bad. Okay… Let's meet at yours after work. I'll call Olly's school and ask if he can stay in the after-school club. They'll feed him and I'll collect him later at six-thirty.'

'Are you sure?'

'Most definitely. Let me show you how sure I am…'

Nell emerged from the linen cupboard with hair that was more messy than when she'd gone in. She tried to straighten it and look normal and presentable, and hoped that her cheeks weren't too flushed by all the naughty things Seth had whispered into her ear.

This thing with Seth was incredible. She'd never felt so desired! Never felt she had such power over a man. It was heady. Powerful. She wanted to enjoy it for what it was. Fun. Exciting. Exhilarating.

But a small voice at the back of her head kept screaming at her. *What are you doing?*

As she settled in at the desk to write out her worksheet, Beth appeared.

'Hey, stranger.'

'Hey.'

'Everything all right? You look a little flushed.'

Nell felt her cheeks flame even more. 'Oh, you know… I got a little upset after not being able to help that little boy in Bed Four. They ended up doing an intraosseous access. I'm okay now.'

Beth sat down next to her. 'Yeah, it's hard watching them do that. But sometimes the patients just don't have the veins for us to work with. You need to let it go. Think of how many kids you get first time, without even an iota of pain.'

'You're right...'

'Listen, me, Lou and the others are meeting for a drink tonight after work. The White Rabbit? You know it? Why don't you join us there? There's a quiz on. We could make a decent team and it would take your mind off today. Grand prize is a meat hamper!'

Nell laughed. 'What am I going to do with a meat hamper?'

'Share it? Come on—what do you say?'

It sounded fun, but she had other plans with Seth...tempting plans...and she didn't want to cancel them. Not one bit.

'Thanks, but I can't tonight.'

'Why not?' Beth said in a whiny voice. 'You never go out! Come on! It'll be good for you!'

'I can't because I'm meeting someone.'

Beth raised an eyebrow. 'The guy?'

She must have blushed, because suddenly Beth was all excited.

'You're meeting a guy! Oh, come on—spill! Who is he? It's someone here, isn't it?'

'Why would it be someone from here?'

'Because this is our only dating pool! So who is he? Do I know him?'

'You don't know him,' she lied, hating herself for lying, but not wanting to have gossip spread about her on the ultra-fast hospital grapevine just yet.

She wanted to keep all the pleasure to herself and not have it sullied by whispers and gossip. Was that wrong? She didn't think so. Because right now what she had with Seth was fun and exciting and it was early days. Keeping it just between them would help the magic last longer. And it was Christmas. Traditionally the hardest time of the year for her. And now suddenly, because of Seth, it was a little bit brighter. A little bit better. Was it wrong to want to hold on to that happiness?

'Damn! Well, he'd better be amazing, because you're missing out on what will be an amazing night.'

Nell smiled. 'Oh, don't worry. I won't be missing out at all.'

'Don't go?' she said, when Seth looked at his watch and said he needed to leave.

He squeezed her against his bare chest as

they lay in her bed. 'I don't want to, but I have to go and fetch Olly.'

'I know. I just… I don't want this to end. I like the cuddling.'

'Just the cuddling?'

She laughed and looked up at him. 'All of it.'

He kissed the tip of her nose. 'Good.'

He rolled out from under her, stood and began to dress. She couldn't help but lie there and admire him. His taut muscles. His flat stomach. His arms. How good his backside looked as he slid on jersey boxers.

'I have a whole afternoon free tomorrow and so do you. I checked. Why don't we spend it together? We could go into town, do some Christmas shopping, then spend an hour or two here before I have to pick up Olly from school. It's his last day tomorrow before they break up for the school holidays.'

'Will I get to see you when Olly's on holiday?'

'Absolutely.' He began to button his shirt. 'Granny is always happy to keep an eye on him. She couldn't do it today, because she was off playing bridge with some friends, but she generally looks after him when I work. The staff help, too.'

'Okay. Christmas shopping in town sounds fun.'

'Great.' He scooted over to give her one

last kiss. 'Have I told you today how amazing you are?'

Nell smiled happily. 'No, you haven't.'

'Well, you are. Amazing. Beautiful. Talented. *Bendy*.' This last was said with a grin and a kiss.

She laughed. 'Go. You'll be late.'

He checked his watch one last time. 'I'll see you tomorrow.'

'You will. Now, go!'

Seth blew her a kiss and disappeared, grabbing his jacket from the back of her bedroom chair before doing so.

As the front door to her flat slammed shut she felt herself sag in disappointment. He had gone. The flat suddenly seemed so empty without him there. How quickly she had become used to his presence.

Stretching her hand out across the sheets, where he had lain, she could already feel them becoming cooler. She rolled over, grabbed his pillow and inhaled his scent and groaned.

Seth had been amazing. Worth waiting for. He had taken her to heights that she had never believed possible. The first time they'd both been so excited that it had been over in a matter of minutes. But the *second* time... The *third* time... Those had been masterclasses in sex and foreplay.

Seth had known how to bring her to the edge of the precipice and then, just as she'd thought she might explode, just as she'd thought she might fall, tease her in another way. Another place. Until her entire body was screaming with need. Only then would he give her what she desired. It had seemed only fair to do the same to him in return.

God only knows what my neighbour thinks all that noise was.

Would she be able to look Mrs Goodleigh in the eye ever again?

For now, she was quite content to lie naked in bed, staring at the ceiling and thinking of all the things that Seth had done to her body. It would keep her going until she saw him again. She wanted him back here with her. So she was no longer alone.

Is that why I'm enjoying him being here? So I'm not alone?

Christmas was such a difficult time of year for her. What if she was just using Seth to blot out the pain she felt? Because when she was with him she stopped thinking about the world. Stopped thinking about her pain over Lucas and how alone in the world she felt. How isolated.

Seth changed all that.

Or…was it something more?

* * *

His last job for the day was to check on a post-operative young lady called Laura Kemp, who had spiked a fever. Her temperature had been steadily rising over the last two hours, after a long and complicated arm surgery to remove a benign growth just twenty-four hours ago.

As he stood by her bed, the nurse, Lou, took Laura's temperature again. 'One zero two point four,' she said, looking at him grimly.

'Okay, let's get her on some antibiotics. I also want full bloods done and a urine sample—just to make sure we're not missing something. And could we get a swab from her surgical site?'

'Of course.'

'I'm going to be away this afternoon, but Dr Peters will be on duty from lunch, so I'll fill him in on Laura's situation when we do the handover. Hourly obs, please, Nurse.'

'Of course,' she said again.

He typed his directions onto the portable tablet that he carried with him, so that Laura's notes would be instantly updated. 'Okay... I've got ten more minutes and then I'm gone. Anyone else you need me to check before I hand over my patients?'

'Amadi is about to leave. Do you want to say goodbye?'

'Of course! I've got him something. It's in my locker. Hang on, I'll go and fetch it.'

He went to his locker and pulled out the gift he'd wrapped earlier, then headed to Amadi's ward, where he was sitting dressed in the chair beside his bed as his aunt gathered all his belongings and his TTOs—drugs and forms *to take out.*

'Amadi! My friend! How are you feeling? Big day!' Seth shook the young boy's hand.

'I am happy.'

'Good. Good! I've got you a little something for later...when you're better.' He passed over the gift.

'What is it?' asked Amadi in his beautiful accent.

'You'll have to open it to find out.'

Amadi ripped open the packaging and then beamed a huge grin. 'A cricket bat! And a ball!'

Seth grinned at the delight on the young boy's face. 'So you can practise when you're better.'

'Thank you so much!'

'Hey, it was my pleasure. We're going to miss you around here.'

'Thank you.'

He chatted with Amadi and his aunt for a little while, and then it was time for them to go. He waved them off, noting that Nell stood in the doorway too, giving the young boy a little wave.

Seth went to stand by her as Amadi left. 'It's always good to see them leave looking so happy.'

'It is. That was a nice thing you did. The bat and ball.'

'Oh, anyone would have done the same.'

She looked at him. 'Not everyone. Are you ready to go? I'm done for the day.'

'I'll just grab my things.'

Nottingham City Centre was bedecked with Christmas lights and festive music blared from every shop they passed. One minute they'd be singing along to a song about someone driving home for Christmas, the next a merry jingle about a reindeer with a red nose.

They entered a shop selling soaps and bath bombs. It had an overwhelming sweet scent. Nell bought a gift box of bath bombs that looked like Christmas puddings and tree baubles for her mother. Seth bought his grandmother a similar gift box, but this one was filled with whipped soaps that were meant to be moisturising for dry skin.

Next they entered a bookshop, because Seth wanted to get Olly some books. Apparently the little guy liked to read. Nell felt weird, going with him into the children's fiction section. She'd not been in one since losing Lucas, and it felt strange to be there. On a display table was one of the last books she'd ever bought for him. The story of a lonely astronaut who met an alien and became friends with it. Seeing it struck her quite hard, and she thought she must have gasped, because suddenly Seth was asking her if she was all right?

'That book… The one with the spaceman on the front… I bought it for Lucas just before he…'

He reached out for her hand and brought it to his mouth, kissing it. 'Shall we go?'

'No! You must get something for Olly. It's why we're here.'

'But if this hurts you…'

'I'm okay. Just shocked, that's all.'

She was glad of his hand in hers and though he picked a few books off the shelves to look at, he didn't let go.

It felt good to be holding his hand. In public! Something that had never happened with Blake… It was as if Seth wanted the world to know that he was with her. That she was his. She kind of liked that. Even if it was all new and fresh and fun, and she had no idea where it might lead. She never let herself think of the future, because then she'd feel afraid of what she might lose next. It was best to just stay in the present and just enjoy it.

Seth picked up a book about a knight. 'Think he'd like this?'

'I don't know.' How could she know? She didn't know Olly. Not really. They'd had a pizza together. That had been it. But he had played a knight in his school play. 'Maybe. What's he into?'

'Knights. Dragons. Quests.'

Lucas had liked the same things. 'Well, probably he would, then.'

'I'll get it. And once we're done here, let's grab a drink.'

'Okay.'

Seth paid for the book and then they went upstairs to the part of the bookshop that had a café where they could sit. They both ordered hot chocolate, with whipped cream and marshmallows. Nell opted for a spiced ginger one that was on special offer.

'This is delicious!' she said, as they sat down at the one remaining table, which had just been cleared and wiped down by a member of staff.

'It's good to sit down. My feet are killing me today,' said Seth.

'Mmm... Want to try mine?' She proffered her drink and he took a sip.

'Nice. Not too spicy, but a nice after-kick with the ginger. Warming...'

'Have you thought about what else you might get your gran and Olly for Christmas?'

'Olly wants a new bike. We left his old one behind in Devon, because it was getting too small for him, so I've ordered a new one. I'm hoping it will arrive in time. Granny's always difficult to buy for. She's got everything.'

'That's how I feel when I buy stuff for my mum and dad.'

'You don't talk too much about them.'

'They live so far away, so it's mainly phone calls or video calls. Mum was hit hard by losing Lucas. He was her first and only grandson. She struggles sometimes...feels like she's lost her role as grandma.'

'I can't even begin to imagine what it must be like to lose a child. You see it happen to parents at the hospital on occasion, and though you try to be there for them to lean on there's that professional distance that keeps you safe, you know? Even though it's upsetting, and you might shed a tear or two with them... I can't imagine what it would be like to lose Olly.'

'It's not something you can imagine, is it? You know growing up that you will one day lose your grandparents, and then your parents, but you never imagine you'll ever have to face losing a child. Especially one so young. When it does happen…' She was lost for a moment, thrown back to those dark days of grief and pain. 'It's difficult to accept. Like it can't be happening. Not for real.'

He reached across the table and took her hand in his. 'You are so strong.'

She looked down at their hands, felt a warmth inside that did not come from the spiced ginger hot chocolate. This was what she'd always wanted! A man not afraid to show affection in public. A man who admired her and cherished her. A man who could rock her world in bed and be just as hungry for her body as she was for his. A man who made her smile. A man who listened to her cares and her woes without one eye on the clock.

Dr Seth James was simply amazing, and she was so lucky to have him in her life.

I'll have to get him an amazing Christmas present.

'Thank you,' she said. 'So are you. I think we've both been tested where loss is concerned.'

'Ain't that the truth?'

They drank their hot chocolate, and Nell reached across the table with a napkin to wipe the cream moustache from Seth's upper lip, laughing. It felt good. Free. Fun. It was a feeling she could get used to. She enjoyed his company. It made her feel good just being around him.

'Where to next?' she asked.

'Jewellery shop. I think I might get Granny a new necklace or some earrings.'

'Perfect. I'll get the same for Mum,' agreed Nell.

The jewellery shop was sparkling with silver and gold decorations when they got there. Oversized baubles bigger than beach balls hung in the window, and up above, from the ceiling, hung silver and ice-white snowflakes. The necklaces, earrings, rings and bracelets glittered beneath the shop lights in their pristine glass cases, so that it was hard to know where to look first. It was a veritable feast for the eyes.

'Oh, look at that!' said Nell, admiring a rose gold bracelet with charms on it like a cluster of flowers.

'Gorgeous. Think you'll get that for your mum?'

Nell looked at the price tag and winced. It was almost a month's salary. 'I couldn't afford that. No, she'll have to make do with something considerably cheaper. Ooh, those are nice!' She pointed at the next case where a pair of gold earrings lay. Studs, with small dangling cascades attached, and on the end of each one a small round ball, like the stud above. They were simple, without being too busy, and just the kind of thing her mum might wear. They were an affordable price, too.

It was a while before a shop assistant became free and she could ask to look at them more closely, and Seth wandered off to look at the other display cases. Up close, she could see that the gold studs had a pattern printed on them, which made them even prettier.

'I'll take those, please,' she said.

As she waited for the assistant to wrap her purchase, she turned around to see where Seth was. He was on the opposite side of the store, admiring the necklace he held in his hands, before nodding at the assistant who was serving him. The assistant, a young woman with slicked-back dark hair and a tight black turtleneck jumper that emphasised her perfect figure, smiled and fluttered her eyelashes at Seth.

He didn't appear to notice, and Nell smiled to herself before turning back to pay for her mum's earrings.

She felt so incredibly lucky right now.

This Christmas was shaping up to be one that she might even enjoy. Since losing Lucas, she did her Christmas shopping from home, buying online. This was the first time she'd ventured out into the world to do it for herself. It felt good, to be doing this with Seth. He was like a safety blanket. A constant reassuring presence at her side. She was *with* someone.

But how long would it last?

She didn't want to think about that at all.

After Christmas shopping they went back to Nell's place and fell straight into bed and each other's arms.

Seth felt great, just lying there, holding Nell in his arms, entwined around each other. It brought him a peace that he'd not felt for a very long time.

'What are you thinking about?' she asked him.

'About this. You.' He felt himself stir and knew that she could feel it too.

Nell laughed. 'I can tell! You want to go again?'

'Always, with you.'

She played with his chest hair with her fingers. 'Me too.'

'I wish I'd met you earlier.'

'You do?'

'Yeah… I guess you could say I was lost in the wilderness for a while, after losing Dana. I was beginning to accept that I'd always be alone. And I thought I was okay with that. But since knowing you I've come to realise that I was never okay with that. Being alone means never truly being happy.'

He felt her smile upon his chest. 'I make you happy?'

'You know you do.'

She looked up at him. 'You make me happy, too.'

'Good.' He kissed the top of her head and gave her a little squeeze.

'Do you ever worry about what the future holds?' she asked.

'I don't know. Maybe. Sometimes. What about you?'

'I try not to think about it. It scares me. All the stuff that hasn't happened yet. Losing Lucas was the worst thing ever, and now I know what real pain is I'm scared of losing anyone else. Losing Lucas broke me, and I can't be broken again. I'm not sure you can fit that many broken pieces back together.'

'I get that.'

They were quiet for a moment or two. Thinking.

'Losing Dana… It made me realise that happiness is fleeting. So when it does come you should grab hold of it, because you never know how long you've got it for.'

'You mean like this?'

He felt her hand drift lower and take hold of him, begin to stroke.

'Hmm… Maybe,' he said, feeling his body awaken once again.

Her touch had the power to revive more often than he'd ever believed possible. It was as if he simply couldn't get enough of her. As if his body wanted to be fed the drug that was Nell Bryant over and over again. Like an addict.

He rolled her onto her back and lay atop her, staring down into her eyes. 'Let's just enjoy the happiness we have in the present and not worry about what's ahead for us, okay?'

'Why would we worry? It's good.'

'I know. But if it keeps being good, then it's going to lead to it being a proper relationship, and then we'll have to start asking ourselves some pretty deep questions about what we want from this.'

Had he felt her stiffen beneath him? Just slightly? But he'd had to mention it, because she'd lost her son. Her precious son. And he came with one. If they got serious, she'd have to consider the possibility that she'd have a greater role in Olly's life than she'd thought about. And that scared him, too.

What would Olly think about him bringing Nell into their lives? He'd hate to think that

Olly might believe he was trying to replace his mother. He might not be ready.

Seeing the look of uncertainty and, yes, even fear, in Nell's eyes panicked him, so he kissed her. Once. Twice. Three times. He didn't want to think of scaring her away. He didn't want to imagine it. He wanted what they had now. The fun. The joy. The happiness.

'But we don't need to worry about that now,' he whispered into her ear, before he began to trail his lips down her body.

He wanted to take them both to another place. A place where they didn't need to think. A place where she *couldn't* think and nor could he.

He didn't want to fill their minds with what-ifs, because he didn't want to spoil this.

He just wanted to escape into ecstasy.

It was simpler there.

When Seth left for the evening she stood in the doorway to her flat, dressed only in her bathrobe, her body aching deliciously as she kissed him goodbye. She was smiling and waving as he stepped into the lift, but the second the lift doors closed, taking him from view and whisking him down to the ground floor, her smile faltered.

She closed the door and leaned back against it, her mind filled with what he'd said.

'But if it keeps being good, then it's going to lead to it being a proper relationship, and then we'll have to start asking ourselves some pretty deep questions about what we want from this.'

He'd thought about that. Did it worry him? It must do. And, worst of all, he was right. They *would* have to start asking themselves some pretty deep questions about this. For example, could she accept the fact that he came with a little boy of his own? Olly would be a daily reminder of all that she had lost in Lucas. He also came with a manor house, a rich history and a title—a type of living that she just wasn't used to.

Were they fooling themselves right now? The sex was great, it was true, but a relationship couldn't be built on just sex. There had to be more to it than that. And, yes, she enjoyed his company—they could talk and laugh about anything—but had they ever talked about anything serious? Like people in a real relationship would?

Nell headed into the kitchen and opened the fridge, hoping for some inspiration as to what to cook for dinner. No doubt Seth would go back to the Manor and have a meal cooked for him. They lived such different lives. Came from two different worlds. Were their differences insurmountable? Were they fooling themselves that everything would be fine whilst they hid their relationship from reality?

Neither of them had told anyone that they were sleeping together. Olly didn't know. The Dowager, Seth's grandmother, didn't know. Their friends didn't know. What would happen when everyone found out and the real world entered to complicate everything? There were so many unanswered questions that were beginning to trouble her.

And this is why I don't allow myself to think of the future. Because it just upsets me.

There was a lonely chicken breast in the fridge, and half a jar of sweet and sour sauce. She knew she had rice in the cupboard...

That would have to do.

The next couple of days were strange ones for Nell. She saw Seth at work and they stole kisses in linen cupboards...secret smiles during handovers. Occasionally their hands would brush one another's as they passed by a patient's bed. Each touch, each kiss, was a reminder of the happiness he brought to her, but also a stark reminder that they would soon have to face reality.

They were good together. That much was clear. He made her smile. He made her sigh. The way she felt when she was with him was something that she couldn't clearly articulate because there were not enough superlatives in the world for that. But she couldn't help thinking that she'd gone from a relationship with a man who couldn't show love in public to a relationship with a man who was afraid to show love in public. Because if he did, everything would change.

Keeping their relationship secret was the only thing that kept it alive in its current state, and she wanted to remain in that blissful state for as long as she could. Because losing Seth... Just the mere idea of that was enough to make her want to hide from the world and its cruelty. That it should give her a taste of such fine happiness only to take it away again.

So as Christmas Eve arrived Nell went about her work as normal, determined to stay busy, determined to keep her head down, knowing she wouldn't be spending Christmas with Seth. He would be at the Manor, with his grandmother and his son, whereas she would be home alone.

She popped in to see Ruth, her supervisor, in her office, midway through the shift. 'Hey,

Ruth. I was wondering…do you need me to come in tomorrow? I'm free… I could do it.'

'Christmas Day? No, no. I told you. You've worked the last two Christmases. You deserve to take this year for yourself. Besides, Marie and Owen are in.'

'Oh… Well, what if I swapped a shift with them?'

'Take the day off, Nell! Enjoy Christmas,' Ruth said in a stern voice, yet she was also somehow smiling.

'Okay…'

Maybe she could go to Lucas's grave? Take him some flowers. Take a present for him and leave it there. Just something small. Unobtrusive. Something that wouldn't get stolen.

The ward had a different atmosphere today. Christmas was nearly here and the doctors were trying to safely discharge as many patients as they could. So there were a few empty beds and her beeper didn't go off nearly as much as it usually did, and she actually found herself at a loose end. Determined to do something useful, she headed to Pixie Ward and the small play area and began to tidy up.

There were books all over the floor, rather than in the bookcase, and the dressing up clothes were half off their hangers. One princess outfit was on the floor. The building blocks and the cars were all in disarray.

She spent a good fifteen minutes tidying up, and was busy keeping her mind off all her feelings and the idea of spending Christmas alone in her flat with nothing more than a pathetic attempt to make a turkey dinner for one, when suddenly Beth came looking for her.

'Nell? I need you.'

She stood up. 'What's going on?'

'We've got a patient being sent up from the ER. A young boy who keeps having grand mal seizures. I know you don't normally help with new admissions, but I've just sent Lou and Angel off for a break as it was quiet. Can you help me get him settled?'

'Of course.'

She didn't mind at all. In fact it would be nice to help. She hated having nothing to do.

'Where's Dr James?'

'He had to go and see Dr Soong in Theatre, and the on-call doc is with another patient right now.'

'Okay. Just tell me what you need me to do.'

'I can do the kid, but could you assist the parents? You never know what state they'll be in when they come up here. No one wants their child to be admitted to hospital—and especially not right before Christmas.'

No. They didn't. Nell remembered her own bewilderment at having to rush to a hospital a few weeks before Christmas. Seeing her pale, lifeless son in a hospital bed. He'd looked so small! So helpless! And there'd been nothing she could do to fix it. And no one to hold her hand.

Blake had been there, eventually. But he'd stood opposite her, looking down at Lucas, his jaw rigid and firm. More than anything she'd wanted him to come and stand beside her, clasp her hand. When he hadn't she'd gone to him and taken his hand, but he'd pulled it free, almost as if he was angry at her. As if it was all her fault that their son was in this place.

Parents could turn on one another. She'd seen it many times. Fear would push most people together, but for others it tore them apart. As it had to her own marriage.

There was a beep at the double doors to the ward and Beth responded to it, buzzing through the nurses and the techs from downstairs as they wheeled a boy on a trolley into the ward. Behind them were two parents. A mum and a dad. The mum with a tear-stained face, the father pale and shocked as their son was manoeuvred into a side ward and transferred from the trolley onto the bed.

Nell, feeling their pain and fear, went to

stand by them. 'Hi. I'm Nell. A phlebotomist
and play specialist here on the paediatric floor.
Don't worry, we're going to get him settled and
monitored first, and then the doctors will run
any further tests they might need. Has your
son had seizures before?'

She got her first glimpse of the boy in the
bed and felt rocked to her core. This little boy
looked so like Lucas! The same shock of blond
hair. The same pale skin and freckles over his
nose. He was even wearing a pair of pyjamas
the same as one Lucas had once owned.

The mum began a fresh burst of crying. 'No!
Never!'

The dad put his arm around his partner.
'He's been complaining of headaches for a few
days now. We thought it was just so he could
get out of the last few days of term. We should
have known something was wrong.'

Nell tried not to stare at Lucas's double.
Tried to pull herself out of the shock she was
feeling and be helpful to these two worried
parents. *Lucas had suffered with headaches.*

'You couldn't possibly have known. Did they
do any scans downstairs?'

'Yes, but the results haven't come back yet.
Do you have them here? What do they say?'

'A doctor would have to take a look,' Nell
said, looking away from their son and guid-

ing Mum and Dad towards two plastic seats against the wall. 'What's your son's name?'

'Luke.'

Nell felt her stomach drop to the floor. *Luke?*

'Can I get you guys anything? Tea? Coffee? Some water?'

'Tea would be great, thank you. We've not had time to get anything for hours.'

'Okay, I'll be back in a minute.'

It was such a relief for her to be free of the fear in that room. Free of the trepidation. The hope for good news. The hope to hear that this was all just something and nothing. That it would pass. Or it would be something easily controlled by medication.

But hope could be a terrible thing. Sometimes it blinded you. Sometimes it lured you. And when all hope was gone...

That was the most difficult thing of all.

That little boy, Luke...

She shook her head to clear the image of him in that hospital bed. It was like looking at her own son all over again. Would she have to watch him deteriorate, like she had Lucas?

She'd rushed to the small kitchenette, wiping tears from her eyes with her sleeve, when behind her the door opened.

'Hey, what's the rush?'

Seth.

He would know. He would understand. She turned to him and buried her face in his chest as she cried tears that she'd kept behind barriers for way too long.

'Hey…what's going on?'

She felt his arms surround her, felt his protection and his concern as he began to rub her back and stroke her hair, waiting for her to cry it out. It meant so much, in that moment, that he was there for her, and that he allowed her to experience her emotions without trying to ignore them.

When the torrent finally ended she was able to just stand there, her head against his chest, sniffing gently. 'A boy has just been brought onto the ward. He looks so like Lucas…and his parents…they're so scared… I just felt… And then the mum said his name is Luke. I don't know… You probably think this is silly, but it was like looking at my own son all over again.'

There was a pause whilst he took in all her words. 'I don't think it's silly at all.'

She was so grateful to him right there and then! To not have her feelings dismissed. To not be told she was being silly. Or hysterical. Or over-emotional. Blake had used to accuse her of that kind of thing all the time whenever she got upset. Because he himself was uncomfortable with such a show of emotion.

He couldn't handle it, and had often berated her for behaving in such a way.

'Thank you,' she said. 'I've said I'd make the parents a cup of tea. I don't think they've had anything for hours. They're waiting for scan results, too.'

'Want me to go check on them?'

'Please.'

'Okay.' He kissed the top of her head. 'Meet me at the desk when you've made their drinks. We'll go in together.'

She gave him a thankful smile and set about making the tea, feeling slightly better having let out all the emotion that had been stirring in her ever since she'd laid eyes on Luke and his parents. She still felt apprehensive about going back into that boy's room, but with Seth at her side maybe she could achieve anything?

With the drinks on a tray, she headed out to the nurses' desk, where Seth sat. He was on the phone, his face grim.

She put down the tray and waited for him to get off the phone. 'What is it?'

'Luke's CT scans. Come and take a look.'

Frowning, she headed round to his side of the desk.

She didn't need to be a radiographer or a doctor to understand what was wrong and why Luke was having grand mal seizures. There was a growth in his brain. A large one. Easily the size of an egg.

'A tumour…? That poor boy.'

'I've just spoken to the neurosurgeons. They've taken a look, and want a further MRI to be sure, but they're hoping they can operate to remove it. They're going to come down and talk to the parents with me.'

The parents… Her heart broke for them. It was Christmas! To receive news such as this on Christmas Eve! Any time would be horrible, of course, but at this time of year… She couldn't imagine how they were going to react to this. But at least they would have hope. At least the surgeons thought they could operate.

He had more options than Lucas had had.

'What will you say to them?' she asked.

'I'll just have to be honest. Come on. Let's go get this over with.'

Luke's parents took the news exactly as he'd expected they would. In abject shock and horror, looking at their son as if they couldn't quite believe what was happening to them as a family.

Seth was thankful that Nell was there. She was being a superstar, despite her own upset. Sitting with them…comforting them. Trying as best she could to make them look at the positive side of things.

But she would know, wouldn't she? Exactly how these parents were feeling and what they needed?

Luke had been given anti-seizure medication and had returned from his MRI when the neurosurgical team arrived. He and Nell left the Sanderton family in their capable hands and vacated the room for a breather after what had been an intense couple of hours.

'I feel so sorry for them. They've got a long road ahead,' Nell said.

'Yeah, but at least they have a road. Not everyone gets that chance.'

She looked down at the desk, lost in her own thoughts. 'Yeah…'

He didn't like seeing her so down. Didn't like the idea that he wouldn't get to spend Christmas with her and she'd be home alone in her flat either. She'd had a difficult day. Old memories must have risen from the darkness to torment her.

On impulse, he said, 'Look, I know this is going to sound crazy, and if you want to say no, then please do so, but…why don't you join us for Christmas? We could go to your place and pick up whatever you need. Come and stay at the Manor with Olly and me and Granny.

We often have guests. Olly needn't know what you mean to me just yet. We'll simply say you were going to be alone and it was a nice thing to do for us to invite you.'

She looked at him, smiled. 'Are you saying I mean something to you?'

He leaned forward. Looked right into her chocolate eyes. Whispered, 'You know you do.'

He could see her mulling it over in her mind. Considering her reservations. The down side of such a deal. Surely there weren't that many?

Then she nodded. He saw the resolution in her eyes that she would look for happiness this festive season.

'All right. You've got yourself a deal. Christmas at Elmbridge Manor it is.'

CHAPTER NINE

As Seth drove up the long drive towards Elmbridge Manor, this time in fading sunlight, as the afternoon, turned to dusk and more snow began to fall, Nell felt considerably more relaxed than the last time she'd been driven to his home.

This time she could appreciate all that she was seeing.

Elmbridge was a vast expanse of a building, built out of what looked like sandstone. A myriad windows reflected the dying sun, and the fir trees outside it had all been decorated with white fairy lights and golden baubles. Yellow light shone out from the ground floor and a couple of the first-floor rooms, and she saw some of the staff drawing curtains and preparing for the evening chill.

'I still can't believe you live in a place like this.'

He laughed. 'Only a small part of it. A lot is open to the public, remember?'

'You still can't get away from the fact that our childhoods were vastly different. I played in the street. You had *grounds*.'

Seth shrugged. 'I didn't know any different.'

'Nor me.'

'We're both still good people, though. Does background matter all that much?'

'Maybe… My background holds no expectations of me. While yours…' She paused as she gazed at his impressive home, filled as it was with portraits of past generations. 'Yours has a history and a future to uphold.'

He was quiet for a moment as he pulled the car up in front of the house. Then, 'Does that bother you?'

Of course it did. If she was going to stay involved with him then she needed to think about that. Dana hadn't married him. She'd wanted to keep her independence. Seth had said he'd always felt she had one foot out through the door, ready to bolt, which had bothered him. He would want someone as fully committed to this place as he was, and she didn't know if she was strong enough to carry the burden of Elmbridge past, present and future.

She smiled, hiding her thoughts. 'Of course not.'

'I'm glad.' He turned off the engine and got out of the car.

Nell blew out a breath. This place was imposing. How could it not be? And maybe it wasn't just this place? Maybe it was Seth who was imposing and, like Dana, she was ready to bolt in case things got scary.

Seth came round to open her door for her. She took his hand as she alighted from the vehicle. 'Am I going to get the tour this time?' she asked.

'If you want one. Let's get inside first, and tell Granny and Olly that you're going to be staying with us.'

'Okay...'

She was nervous about spending Christmas with them. She'd not had a family Christmas for a long time, and although she was excited about how they might go about it at Elmbridge, she was worried too. But to not be alone... To not have to sit and watch the King's speech on Christmas afternoon with her meal for one, in an empty flat, listening to her neighbours' merriment all around her...

Everyone was so excited to have snow for Christmas. It wasn't ever a given in the United Kingdom, despite its penchant for bad weather. Usually Christmas only merited cold or rain. But this year they were going to get that white Christmas that so many singers sang about on the radio.

It was going to be a fine time. A time for hope. A time for joy. She needed to try and remember that.

Before they'd left the hospital Nell had called in to say goodbye to Luke's family. Luke's mum had told her that their son was going to go down for surgery immediately, and that the surgeons had high hopes of removing the tumour. And Seth had told her that the neurosurgical team had promised to call him when the surgery was over to let him know how it had gone.

Neither of them had work now until the day after Boxing Day. Hopefully by then Luke would be recovering. Children usually bounced back from surgeries so well—she could only keep her fingers crossed that he would do the same and that after Christmas she would be able to go into his room and see his smile. No more headaches. No more seizures. No worried parents gazing anxiously at their sick son. Maybe they'd even still have time to enjoy Christmas?

Jeffreys appeared at the front door.

'Can you take Miss Bryant's bags up to my room, please?' Seth asked.

Nell turned to look at him, surprised that he'd said that. They'd be sleeping together? She'd just assumed she'd be put in a guest room, like last time. But she didn't mind. There was no need to hide it. The staff would notice more if she didn't sleep in her own room, or caught her creeping back to there before morning. If this was how he wanted to play it, fine—but would he be open with his family? It was one thing to tell them that she'd be staying with them for Christmas, but sleeping in his room…?

As they stepped into the hall with its chequerboard flooring she smiled. It seemed almost familiar! She looked up the sweeping staircase at the portraits and the tapestries and wondered if she'd ever be able to get used to such a place. Would the grandeur ever become normal?

Another staff member arrived to take her coat and she slipped from it with ease, marvelling at how smoothly and efficiently the staff worked at taking care of their guests.

'The Dowager and your son are in the playroom, my lord,' said Jeffreys. 'Shall I let them know you've arrived?'

'Please. And if you could inform them that Miss Bryant—Nell—will be our guest for Christmas? We'll see them later in the dining room, but for now I want to give Nell a tour of the house.'

'Very good, sir.' Jeffreys moved away with

her bags, disappearing through a door behind a suit of armour.

Nell turned to look at Seth and grinned. 'This is crazy!'

He smiled and came closer, wrapping his arms around her and pulling her close. 'What is?'

'All of it! This house...the staff...you. Why did you tell Jeffreys to put my stuff in your room?'

He frowned. 'You want your own room?'

'Well, no. But your gran... Olly... They don't know that we're together, do they?'

'Not yet, no.'

'Won't you have to tell them? Properly? Face to face? Olly will need it explained to him and...'

Seth kissed her, stopping the flow of words, the flow of worry and concern. The press of his lips against hers very quickly absolved her of all worry as she sank into the wonder of his kiss, and when it was over she was almost breathless.

'Everything will be fine,' he whispered.

'Will it? Sometimes I wonder.'

'This scares you? This place?'

She nodded.

'Why?'

'It's just so much. It's like I can't take it all

in. And there's also what you said before about us needing to ask ourselves some questions if this gets serious...'

'And is it? Serious?'

She nodded. 'Don't you think so? I need to know what you want from me. What you expect if this goes any further. It's not just you and me, Seth. There's a little boy involved here too, and we have to think of him.'

'I do think of him. Always.'

'I know you do. As I think of Lucas—even though he's not here any more. If you tell your family I'm your girlfriend, or whatever you want to call me, then Olly will... Olly will think I'm trying to take the place of his mum, and I'm not sure if I'm ready for that.'

Seth nodded and let out a sigh. 'I know. It worries me too. He's been through so much... I don't want him being hurt again.'

'And I don't want to be the one to hurt him.'

He smiled. 'You could never do that. But let's not worry about all this yet. It's Christmas. Let's just enjoy being together for now. I'll let Olly and Granny know it's something new, nothing established just yet. Then there'll be no expectations.'

'There's always expectations, Seth.'

He took her hand. 'I know. But for now let's push them to one side and just enjoy being here together. I want you to have a good Christmas. I don't want you to be alone with your thoughts. And if you want to cry then that's fine too. Just cry on me, okay? Let me be here for you—that's all I ask.'

That meant something. That meant a lot.

And maybe he was right. Maybe she was worrying excessively when she didn't need to be doing that yet.

Not here. Not at this time of year.

'Okay.'

Seth reached for her hand and led her down a corridor and through a set of double doors. They passed through a small interconnecting corridor that was plainly decorated, then turned a corner and came to another door.

'This is the side of the house that's open to the public,' he said, before opening it and leading her out into another vast reception hall, with the same kind of chequerboard floor. But this time all its adornments—the pictures and the tapestries—had little white cards beneath, filled with information about what the object was. Where it came from, who commissioned it, and its place in Elmbridge's heritage.

There was a pair of ornate vases at the base of a sweeping staircase. Mainly white, but patterned with large flowers of pink and cream and adorned with gold leaf. The card beneath said that the vases had been a gift from a grateful Albert, Prince Consort, who had stayed at the house in 1846.

'Prince Albert? Queen Victoria's husband?'

'Yes. I believe he stopped here once for a hunting weekend, to break up his journey to Scotland. He was very good friends with one of my great-grandfathers.'

'Wow…'

She knew she shouldn't be surprised. Elmbridge was a great house, and in the past would have been a perfect place for people of importance to stay. To think that royalty had stayed here…in the very same building where she would lay her head tonight.

'Are you still friends with royalty?'

He laughed. 'Not as much as you might hope. I know people who are third and fourth cousins of the King, and we see each other on occasion, but it's just like when you and your friends get together. We're all just people at the end of the day. We're nothing special.'

Of course he'd think that. Those were the circles he moved in. Nell could claim no knowledge of any cousins! Her friends were Beth, Angel and Lou. Nurses. Doctors. X-ray technicians. Physiotherapists. If her friends visited her place the only things they left behind were take-out containers and empty wine bottles.

As he led her around the parts of Elmbridge open to the public, it really began to hit home how different they were and how they came from entirely different worlds.

But she admired Seth. He had not sat back on his laurels, believing that his title meant that all he had to do was manage his tenant farmers and lord it over the local village. He'd got himself an education. Had gone to university. Studied medicine. Become a doctor—a paediatrician. And he worked for the NHS—he wasn't a private doctor. He was devoted to his son and was raising him without nannies. He was kind and considerate and hot and—

Oh, boy, am I in trouble!

She held his hand as they wandered through the corridors and rooms. She particularly liked the library, with its green leather sofas, the morning room, with its bright daffodil-yellow walls, and upstairs the Pink Bedroom, where the card on the door informed her that this had once been the bedroom of the notoriously bad-tempered Lady Ethel.

'Why was she so bad-tempered?'

'She wasn't a well woman, by all accounts. Suffered terribly from migraines and couldn't abide loud noise. She used to demand that all the servants in her room wore slippers on their feet, as their shoes clunked too loudly on the wooden floors. There's a portrait of her on the stairs. I'll show you when we go back down.'

They climbed to the next floor. Here were all the guest rooms. Smaller than the family bedrooms, but only just. There was the Hedley Room, the Polly Suite, the Rose Room... Each one decorated tastefully and kept in pristine condition. Some were roped off by thick red rope hung between brass posts. As was a small staircase. Another door.

'Why can't we go past those?'

'Repairs and maintenance. An old house like this one occasionally springs a leak. To get ahead of any real damage we close off certain areas on a regimented cycle each month, to maintain what's there and preserve its history. Do you want to see the old staff quarters at the top of the house? Jeffreys and the others live in the village now.'

'Oh, yes, please!'

Seth led her up a narrow staircase and opened the door at the top into a narrow corridor. This one wasn't decorated as beautifully as the rest of the house. It was simply painted white. There were no paintings, no tapestries. Just the occasional narrow window with a candle on the ledge, or an old oil lamp or two.

The doors to the servants' rooms had no cards. Each room was plain and simple. A bed. A wardrobe. A table and chair. In one there might be a pile of books next to the bed. In another a piece of embroidery, as if the owner had just set it down to go and get a cup of tea, or something.

'It's a different world. They'd work so hard downstairs and then come up to this.'

'I know. But that was the way back then.'

'You still have staff today.'

'Only because it would be nigh on impossible to maintain this house on our own. And the public have expectations, too. They expect a house like this to have staff. I like to think I look after them as much as they look after me. The pay is good. The hours reasonable. I like to think of them as old friends, really.'

'But doesn't all this get a bit too much? You work so hard at the hospital and yet you still have to deal with all this. Your home being open to the public, employing staff, maintaining the grounds and the house, budgeting, overseeing tenants, business meetings...'

'I have managers and I delegate. A lot,' he added with a rueful smile.

'And are you a good employer, Seth? I mean, are you a kind boss?'

'I'd like to think so. You are, of course, at

liberty to ask any of my staff if they're happy. I can assure you that I don't crack a whip.'

She smiled at his joke and remembered Ava, the maid, telling her how Lord Elmbridge was a brilliant boss. 'I should hope not. And Olly... he'll have to take all this on when it's his turn?'

'I won't ever force him to do anything he doesn't want to. If he decides to become an actor or an astronaut or a busker in the street, I will support him and simply arrange for staff to take care of the estate in his stead. And when he becomes the next Lord Elmbridge, then I'll make sure he'll be ready for that, too.'

She nodded. 'You're a good dad.'

'Thanks. I'm trying to be.' He paused for a moment, then glanced at his watch. 'It's nearly dinnertime. We ought to go down and get changed for dinner, and then say hello to Olly and Granny.'

'And you're sure they won't mind me being here?'

She was very aware that Christmas was a time for families to be together. The James family had such a long and distinguished line, and she was intruding on their private time. They already shared so much with the public... shouldn't Christmas be just for them?

'How could they?' He lifted her hand to his lips and kissed it. 'Come on, let's go down.'

* * *

'You remember Nell?' Seth stepped back so Nell could step forward to say hello to his grandmother once again.

The two women shook hands.

'Of course! Seth very rudely called you a leech the last time you were here. I do hope he's stopped doing that?' His grandmother turned to look at him with one eyebrow raised.

'He most certainly has.' Nell laughed, glancing at him.

'Olly? You remember Nell, don't you? She came to see you at your show and we went for pizza.'

His son nodded. 'You said you weren't Daddy's girlfriend,' the little boy said, much to her embarrassment.

His great-grandmother chuckled. 'Oh, yes, I remember Oliver mentioning that you'd gone out with a lady,' she said with a twinkle in her eye. 'You didn't say it was Nell.'

'Didn't I?' Seth grinned and winked at her.

The wink told his grandmother that she knew full well why he hadn't mentioned it—in case she started to play matchmaker. Well, he didn't need that. He'd been able to start a relationship with Nell without his grandmother's interference, thank you very much, and now it was teetering on the edge. Neither of them knew where it was going. He knew where he wanted it to go, but he still wasn't sure whether he was ready for it.

'You must sit beside me at dinner, Nell. Tell me all that you've been up to,' his grandmother said, as Seth helped pull out chairs for the ladies to sit.

Nell settled obligingly next to her, as requested, opposite Seth and Olly.

They were in the grand dining room, at the big dinner table. This one was capable of seating up to thirty dinner guests, and though it always seemed silly to sit and gather at just one end of it, it was the nicest room to have dinner in. There was a crackling fire behind them and there was something about the room that felt intimate, despite its size.

'Not much, I'm afraid,' said Nell. 'Mainly working.'

'The bane of many a life.'

'Yes, but if you love what you do, then it's not really a problem.'

'And do you? Love what you do?' asked his grandmother.

'I do. I work with a great team, which makes it easier.'

'But it must be hard, working with all those sick children. It must break your heart sometimes. Seth doesn't say much about it, but sometimes he comes home with a dark, sad look in his eyes and I know it must have been a difficult shift.'

He caught Nell's eye. She'd had a difficult day today, with that young boy Luke. He would still be in surgery... He hoped it was going well.

'It can do, yes.'

'But your friends and family get you through it?' his grandmother persisted.

Nell nodded.

'Tell me about your family, Nell. Could you not make it to them for Christmas?'

'Granny...!' he warned.

'I'm just asking, Seth!'

'Well, maybe Nell doesn't want to talk about her family.'

'Nonsense. Everyone loves to talk about the members of their family. The weird one. The drunk one. The embarrassing one. Come on, Nell—I bet you've got some tales to tell. Everyone has!'

He could see the discomfort in Nell's eyes. The first course hadn't even been served yet and his grandmother had grasped Nell with her talons and would not let go. Not now that she suspected there was more to his and Nell's relationship than she'd first believed.

'It's okay, Seth. I don't mind. My parents

live quite far away from here. They did invite me for Christmas, but I would have needed to take too much time off work, which I can't afford to do.'

'Any siblings?'

'No.'

'And you and my Seth have been getting along?' his grandmother asked with a cheeky smile.

'Yes, we have.'

Some of the staff arrived then, walking into the room with an air of grandeur as they prepared to serve the first course. He saw that Cook had made her special chicken liver pâté, and was serving it with strips of sourdough toast. Another secret recipe that she guarded carefully.

'This is lovely,' Nell said.

'It's one of Cook's favourites,' said his grandmother. 'She always makes it on Christmas Eve. I'm afraid we're a family rather steeped in tradition.'

'And history. Seth gave me a tour of the half of the house open to the public. It's an amazing place you have here.'

'Where do *you* live, if you don't my asking?' his grandmother asked, probing for information again.

'Nowhere as palatial as this! I live in a flat.

It's quite small. Barely enough room to swing your arms.'

'Hmm…'

Thankfully, his grandmother went quiet as she delved into her pâté and toast.

Seth sent Nell a look that tried to apologise for his nosy grandmother. But he should have expected it, really. This was the first woman he had brought home since Dana, and although his grandmother had loved Dana, she'd always disliked the fact that Dana never wanted to marry. It had gone against all her own beliefs. That Elmbridge needed its Lord to walk its Lady up the aisle and place a ring on her finger.

As if on cue, his grandmother spoke again. 'What are your thoughts on marriage, Nell?'

Seth winced as Nell choked on a piece of sourdough and set down his own toast. Dabbing at his mouth with a napkin, he looked at his grandmother.

'That's enough, now. Nell didn't come here to be quizzed.'

And he didn't need his grandmother scaring her off when she was nervous enough as it was. All those questions she'd asked on the tour… He wished he had answers for her, but the truth of the matter was that he just didn't know. This was scary for him, too. Bringing her here. Admit to his grandmother that they might have something between them. That he might be taking a step away from his past and further into the future.

Nell was right. This wasn't just about them, but Olly, too, and he had to get this right. He didn't want Olly to be upset in any way shape or form.

'Seth, she came here to be part of our family Christmas. All I'm doing is finding out a little more about her. It's hardly the Spanish Inquisition, dear boy.'

'Marriage is a fine concept,' answered Nell. 'If two people truly love each another and have the respect for one another that they deserve. They shouldn't be married if they don't intend to make the other person happy for the rest of their life.'

'A good answer!' His grandmother smiled. 'And an answer that sounds as if it has a story behind it.'

Nell smiled back at her. 'I was married once. Divorced now. My husband was not the man he first appeared to be, and he married me not because he wanted to make me happy for the rest of my life, but because I was pregnant with his child and he thought it the dutiful thing to do. So did I, in a way. I thought we could make it work because of the baby. That we owed it to our child to try and make it work.'

Seth looked at his grandmother and then at Nell. He'd not known that about Nell and her husband. But he could imagine it. Her trying to do the right thing by her son by giving him a dad. By being a traditional family unit. Trying daily to make it work between them but struggling. Because marriage was hard enough when you loved someone deeply. When that love was conditional it was more difficult still. He admired her even more than before. Putting her child first, before it was even born, and trying to give her son the family she'd believed he needed.

'You have a child?' his grandmother asked.

Nell's eyes darkened.

'*Gran*. No!' he warned.

But his grandmother was like a dog with a bone, and she was not willing to give up on her juicy titbit. 'You have a child?' she asked again, but this time more gently, as if sensing something awful was about to be shared.

'I had a son. His name was Lucas. He died three years ago.'

His grandmother reached out to take Nell's hand, enveloping it with her own fragile, liver-spotted ones. 'My dear, I'm so sorry. He must have been very young when he died?'

Nell nodded, unable to speak.

Beside him, Olly crunched loudly into his toast, oblivious to the tension in the room.

'You must miss him every day. Tell me about him. What was he like?'

Nell glanced at his grandmother in surprise. She'd told him once that she didn't like to mention that she had a dead son to people because normally they'd act as if they were extremely uncomfortable and would change the conversation, or simply walk away as quickly as they could without seeming rude. She'd said hardly anyone asked her to tell them about him.

'He was beautiful. Funny, in a dry way. I often used to say that he was an old soul in a young body. He had this adult way of speaking that just used to make me laugh.'

Nell's eyes glistened as he watched her from across the table.

'We had this calendar on the kitchen wall that had a "Word of the Day" on it and a description of what it meant. Every day Lucas would try to find a way to shoehorn that word into a conversation.'

She smiled and Seth thought she'd never looked more beautiful.

'He was stoic. Wouldn't complain if he fell over and grazed his knee…or bumped his leg and gave himself a bruise. He liked cartoons and cuddly toys. He liked to help me bake cakes. He liked chasing butterflies in the back garden, when we had one, and he wanted a dog so badly. We never got one, because my husband said he was allergic.'

There was silence around the table then. Except for Olly's chewing.

'He sounds like the most wonderful little boy. Do you have a picture?'

Nell nodded and reached for her phone from her back pocket.

His grandmother and Nell spent a few moments scrolling through her pictures. Laughing and smiling. At one point, his grandmother laid her head against Nell's, as if in solidarity. It was a familiarity that he'd not expected.

Maybe he'd been wrong. Maybe his grandmother had not been questioning Nell to try and decide if she was good enough for him, but was instead questioning her to find a way she could connect with her? He knew that his grandmother had lost a baby once…a miscarriage. But back then those sorts of things had never been spoken about. You were expected to just get on with life and leave it in the past.

But you never forgot. How could you?

'From now on, every time we meet, tell me something new about Lucas,' his grandmother was saying now. 'I want to remember him with you.'

Nell nodded and threw her arms around his grandmother. 'Thank you,' she whispered, her eyes wet with tears.

His grandmother was an amazing woman. One of a kind. He must never forget that.

And Nell? With every moment he found himself admiring her more and more. For her quiet strength. Her fortitude. Her kindness and her huge heart.

Was he falling in love with her?

He thought that maybe he might be. He could imagine her at this table. In his bed. Walking the halls. Being the new Lady Elmbridge.

But could she see herself as a new mother to Olly? A stepmother?

If she did, or if she didn't…either way scared the hell out of him.

CHAPTER TEN

APPARENTLY THE JAMES FAMILY tradition was that on Christmas Eve, before they went to bed, everyone would open their Christmas stockings. So they sat in the parlour in chairs, around a gently crackling fire, and watched each other open their gifts.

Olly went first, zooming his way through all his little gifts. A remote-controlled car no bigger than his thumb. A small bag of chocolate coins. A torch in the shape of his favourite cartoon character. A computer game. A yo-yo that apparently he'd been begging his dad for, for ages, and a chocolate Santa.

The Dowager had soap and perfume, a pair of soft woolly socks, a box of candied jellies, which were her favourites, and an ornamental brooch.

Seth received socks, gloves, a beard-trimming kit and a large bar of white chocolate.

'I've got you a little something, but you're

going to have to wait until tomorrow,' she said to him.

'And I got you a little something,' Seth said, reaching into his pocket and pulling out a small box that was beautifully wrapped.

'Oh! You didn't have to!'

'Of course I did. Now, open it.'

Feeling all eyes on her, Nell pulled apart the ribbon, gently prised open the taped-down silver paper and pulled out what looked like a jewellery box. Her heart beating fast in her chest, she opened it—and gasped.

It was the rose gold bracelet with flowers that she'd admired in the jeweller's that day they'd gone shopping!

'Oh, Seth! It's beautiful!'

He helped her put it on. Fastening it around her wrist and then giving her a kiss on the cheek.

'Ooh!' said Olly in a sing-song voice, making everyone laugh.

She couldn't believe it. If someone had told her that she'd be enjoying Christmas as part of a family, with a little boy in tow, sitting around a crackling fire in an amazing manor house, she'd have stared hard at them and told them not to be so incredibly ridiculous!

It was wrong, wasn't it? To be sitting here like this? Shouldn't she be at home, in the quietness, mourning the loss of her son? What did this even mean? Was she moving on? She would never forget Lucas—of course not—but should she be smiling? Should she be enjoying herself?

And yet here she was. Feeling a part of things. A part of *them*. Not just as a guest, but as someone who belonged. Someone who'd been welcomed.

And Seth kissing her like that in front of his son... Well, it had only been a peck on the cheek, but it was a sign, wasn't it? Not just to Olly, but also to the Dowager, and maybe even to himself, of just what Nell meant to him. And the fact that he'd bought her this bracelet...

She was falling for him. There was no denying it. Perhaps she was already in love with him? How could she not be? A little part of her most certainly was. She just needed to be brave enough to accept that maybe she was wholeheartedly.

But every time that thought entered her brain she heard Seth's voice that time.

'But if it keeps being good then it's going to lead to this being a proper relationship, and then we'll have to start asking ourselves some pretty deep questions about what we want from this.'

She'd posed some of those questions ear-

lier today and he'd listened. Really listened.
He hadn't dismissed her concerns, because
no doubt he had them himself, but it had all
seemed so overwhelming right then, and so
they'd agreed just to enjoy the present for a
little while and worry about all that other stuff
later.

But what if she couldn't?

Because whether she liked it or not—
whether she liked Olly or not—Seth came
with a little boy in tow. And because of him,
they couldn't mess around. Olly had already
lost one mum...he didn't need to lose a second mum if she ever decided to become that.

Could she?

Be a mum to someone else's son?

She looked at him now, as he sat playing
with his remote-controlled toy car. He was
wearing penguin pyjamas and fluffy slippers,
cross-legged on the floor. Such an innocent.
Such a young boy. And yet he unnerved her.
He was Seth's son, and she knew how much
Seth loved and adored him. How much Seth
had tried to protect him since his mother's un-
timely death.

Up until now, he'd pretty much kept them
apart, except for that one time she'd gone with
Seth to see Olly's show. Now he'd taken the
step of inviting her for a family Christmas.

He'd had her things sent to his bedroom. He'd kissed her in front of him. Seth was making a declaration, wasn't he? Showing the people he loved how much she meant to him. And now this bracelet. This beautiful bracelet that he'd remembered her admiring.

Was this all moving a little too fast?

It had taken her this long even to decide to enjoy the relationship, but now it was starting to become public and she didn't know if she was ready. It was one thing to sleep with Seth, but if this went any further could she step into the role of mother once again? Because mothers loved their children. And if she grew to love Olly—who really was a sweet little boy—then there'd be no turning back. No escape route. If she got scared and left it would upset not only Seth, but Olly, too.

Was she making a mistake in being here?

Had her need not to be alone at Christmas propelled her into this dilemma? Forcing an issue she wasn't ready to confront?

'I have a gift for you,' she repeated. 'But it's upstairs in one of my bags.'

She went to stand, needing a moment or two alone to think, but Seth grabbed her hand and shook his head.

'That's okay. I don't mind waiting until tomorrow,' he said, smiling at her, winking again.

She smiled back.

He had no idea of the turmoil in her brain.

And as she sank back down into her seat she hoped he never would.

'It's late. I'm off to bed. Come on, Oliver! You've stayed up way past your bedtime. Come with me, and we'll go up together,' said his grandmother.

'Goodnight kiss first,' said Seth, kissing a sleepy Olly on his cheek as his grandmother took hold of her great-grandson's hand and led him away.

'Goodnight, all.'

'Night!' said Olly, grabbing his teddy and giving them both a wave.

When they were gone, he heard Nell let out a long sigh.

'Tired?' he asked.

'A bit. It has been a long day. Full of emotional ups and downs.'

'They never tell you that in the recruiting posters, do they? There's always some fresh-faced nurse or doctor standing there, arms folded, in a pristine uniform. Do you think more people would sign up if they showed someone with messy hair, bags under their eyes and a uniform covered in mysterious stains?' He smiled at the thought.

'Probably not...' She rolled her shoulders, tilting her head from one side to the other.

'Here, let me help.'

He went to stand behind her and began to massage the knots from her shoulders. She was incredibly tense. But her little moans and groans as his fingers soothed her sore muscles fed his desire for her.

It *had* been a long day. A whole day in her company when he hadn't been able to touch her the way he'd wanted to. Even at dinner they'd had to sit opposite one another, and then afterwards, opening their gifts before the fire, she'd sat on a chair far away from him, closest to the flames.

He'd found himself staring at her many times, wondering where their relationship was going. He'd thought Nell seemed to be a little on edge, but maybe that was just nerves at being someone's house guest? Or maybe it was something more?

He knew he would be asking a lot of Nell if he decided they were properly a couple. He came with a son, and she'd lost hers. If Nell took him on, then she also took on his little boy. Was she strong enough to do that? Was she ready? It was hard for him, too. He'd never imagined finding someone else he wanted to share his life with, and yet here he was, moving on, losing his heart, imagining what it might be like to go down on one knee to this woman.

Dana had always refused to marry him and he'd told himself he would never propose again—not to anyone. But dammit if Nell didn't make him dream of what might be... And he could imagine himself down on one knee, opening a small box and looking up into her face, asking her to marry him.

He'd thought his love for Dana was something he would never find again, but somehow this love, for Nell was different. Stronger... He didn't want to scare her away. Didn't want to lose her. But at the same time he was terrified of getting close again because he really couldn't bear the idea of having his heart broken all over again.

To love like that...and to lose that love. Was that why he was holding back? Why he kept telling Nell they didn't have to answer those serious questions yet? The ones that kept cropping up time and time again...

'You seem tired. Want to go up too?' he asked as he continued to massage her shoulders, her soft brown hair falling over his hands.

'Yes. I do. Could I grab a shower first? Or do you only have baths here?'

'We have all the modern conveniences a

woman could desire.' He laughed and held out his hand. 'Come on. We'll go up. Maybe I could join you in the shower?'

She smiled. 'Maybe you could. But I'm just going to be quick. Why don't you wait for me in bed? The best things come to those who wait, they say.'

'Okay. I'll wait.'

He didn't want to wait. He wanted to consume her. But he knew he would honour her request.

'What about the fire? Shouldn't we put it out before we go up?'

'Jeffreys will take care of that.'

'No, we should do it. Help out a bit more.'

Afterwards they headed upstairs. He would have loved to have joined her in the shower again, but he figured he'd have plenty of time in the future to do that. Hopefully. She was tired. She probably just wanted to freshen up before getting into bed and then they could enjoy themselves.

He was looking forward to exploring her body again. He was hungry for her. Tonight had gone well. She'd fitted in with his little family unit perfectly. His grandmother loved her, he could tell, and Olly had just accepted that she was there without question. Maybe this was something adults worried about more than kids? Olly was young. Kids adapted better than adults. Grown-ups were the ones who made life complicated.

In his private bathroom, he showed Nell how to operate the shower and change the temperature, and then he closed the door behind her and began to get undressed, ready for bed. He already felt aroused at the thought of what was to come when she came out of the bathroom. He couldn't wait to be with her again. Hold her. Taste her. Feel the tremors in her body as she came, over and over. Her gasps, her sighs...

Each little moment with her like that was a gift in itself. Something he could treasure. Moments he could lose himself in. And he was going to spend Christmas Day with her. And Boxing Day, too, before they had to return to work.

Maybe it would be time, then, to start telling everyone that they were a thing. It was going to be difficult to hide it. Already he believed one or two people might be beginning to suspect. Dr Claridge had made a comment to him. Professor Meyer had raised an eyebrow or two.

Part of him wanted the world to know that he was with Nell. Another part wanted to keep her all to himself and not let anyone else in. But he knew that was impossible.

He heard the shower being turned off and the sound of the shower door opening and closing. He could imagine Nell, wrapped in a towel, and indeed, moments later, she came into his bedroom wearing just that. He wanted to unwrap her and lick off any remaining water droplets. He would be diligent and make sure he didn't miss any, and that would mean a careful exploration of her body...

'What are you thinking about? You've got a strange smile on your face,' she said.

'Thinking about you and all the things I could do to you.'

'Oh, really?' She smiled, releasing her hair from the topknot she'd tied it in and letting it fall over her bare shoulders. It looked slightly damp, but glossy and wild.

'Really...' He took hold of the covers on his bed and drew them back, inviting her in. 'Let me demonstrate.'

She stood there, smiling at him, and then, without breaking eye contact, she reached for her towel and undid the knot, allowing it to drop to the floor. She stood before him completely naked in the soft darkness of the room. A vision. A goddess. And he couldn't bear to be apart from her a moment longer.

He reached for her hand and pulled her, giggling, towards him.

* * *

As she'd stood under the hot spray she'd toyed with the idea of going back into his room and telling him that maybe this was a mistake. Maybe this was going too fast. Maybe she ought to sleep in her own room, whilst she clarified her thoughts?

But the idea of not getting to spend at least one more night with him was too much.

He was just in the next room! And she wasn't ready yet to see the smile on his face falter. Not at Christmas. He'd generously invited her into his family home for Christmas Day, and Christmas Day they would have! In front of Oliver and his grandmother they would be able to control themselves and keep their relationship less obvious, and then… Then she would say she needed to go home. She'd be able to get some space to think about what they were doing and whether she could handle where it was going—because she'd accepted his invitation here without thinking.

She'd just not wanted to be alone, that was all. She had not accepted because she wanted him to think that this relationship might be more than it was. But the truth was, it had already become more than she'd expected. Unexpectedly, he had found his way into her heart.

It would break her to walk away. She knew

that. Just thinking about doing it had caused tears to fall in the shower. She loved Seth. She knew she did. But Seth was part of a package. She couldn't have him without Olly, and she didn't know if she was strong enough to be what Olly needed her to be.

She'd always imagined that if she did meet someone in the future they would take their time. Learn about one another, get used to one another, fall in love with one another. And then, and only then, if their love was true they'd get married? That would be the time to get used to the idea of having another child.

Olly was great. He was sweet and lovely and she'd enjoyed watching him in his school play, and tonight, playing with his little remote control car. He'd even let her have a go with it, and she'd crashed it into the fireplace. But there was a big difference between enjoying moments like that and becoming a potential stepmother.

What am I doing? she had asked herself. *Am I just assuming, here? Seth hasn't even asked me to be Olly's stepmother!*

So she'd shaken off her doubts and her fears and gone into his bedroom, determined to enjoy her Christmas with Seth. And all her worries—along with that insidious voice that

kept whispering to her that she ought to run—
were pushed to the back of her mind.

It would be fine.

It would all be fine.

She'd been dreaming of walking the halls of
Elmbridge with Seth. Holding his hand. Smiling. Laughing. The world had been in slow motion. Seth had wanted to show her something,
and had taken her to the head of the staircase
to see a new painting he'd had commissioned.
There'd been a velvet cloth over it, and when
he'd pulled it off, he revealed an oil painting of
her. Eleanor James. The new Lady Elmbridge.
And when she'd turned there'd been paparazzi,
shouting her name, cameras flashing, screaming questions at her.

'How does it feel to become a mother again?'
'Do you feel like you're replacing your son?'
'Do you think you belong here?'

She'd woken with a start, sweating, gasping, only to find herself in the dark, with Seth
sleeping soundly beside her.

No. I'm not in the dark.

The bedroom door was open. Odd… She felt
sure it had been closed after they'd made love.
But a shaft of light from the hall fell through
the gap. She looked around the room, into the

shadows, and realised that Olly was standing beside her. Staring at her. Clutching his teddy.

The way Lucas had used to.

'O-Olly…what are you doing in here?' she whispered, her heart hammering in her throat.

'I think I heard Santa Claus,' he said in soft tones, clearly not wanting to wake his father.

She stared at him. Lucas had been a light sleeper, too. The slightest sound—a dog barking, a car alarm, a storm—would wake him and he'd come to their room and want to climb into bed with them.

'You need to go back to your room,' she said, more firmly than she wanted to.

But this was freaking her out. He'd found her in his dad's bed!

'Can't I sleep with you?'

No, no, no! She couldn't deal with this. It was all too much! This was exactly what she'd feared!

'Your dad's asleep.'

'He normally lets me, if I can't sleep.'

'Santa won't come if you sleep here.'

'He's already been. The presents are under the tree. I've checked. So, can I get into bed with you?'

There'd been nothing she loved more than those occasions when Blake had been away from home and Lucas had climbed into bed with her, snuggling against her, and she'd wake in the morning to find him starfished across the bed, his hair all mussed and smelling of sleep.

But if she stayed in this bed with both Olly and Seth in it…? That would say something about their relationship that she wasn't ready to face yet!

'Okay. You get in. I'll just go and…erm… get myself a drink.'

She clambered from the bed gently, helped Olly get in and pulled the covers over him, tucking him in without thinking about it.

Seth murmured and rolled over, and she froze, but his breathing remained deep and steady.

'Be quiet and go back to sleep, all right?' she told Olly.

Olly nodded happily from the bed and closed his eyes.

Nell stared down at the two boys. One she most definitely loved and the other… She didn't know. She *liked* Olly. But could she allow herself to love him? And if she did love him, did that mean she'd love Lucas less? No, of course not. Lucas would always be her little boy.

A lump of grief tore through her at the thought that Seth still got to enjoy night-time cuddles with his son when she couldn't, and she quickly gathered the clothes she'd been wearing earlier and rushed from the room, closing the door behind her quietly.

She couldn't bear to stay there a moment longer.

CHAPTER ELEVEN

CHRISTMAS MORNING. His favourite morning. Seth had enjoyed an amazing sleep, and moreover he'd got to share the night with Nell. He rolled over to snuggle with her, to spoon her— only to discover that the body in the bed next to him was considerably smaller than he'd been expecting.

He opened his eyes.

Olly?

Damn. He must have crept into the bed in the middle of the night. Where's Nell?

She must have got up and switched rooms. He could understand why she might not feel comfortable about sharing a bed with his son just yet.

I'll go and find her in a minute.

'Hey, sleepyhead.'

Olly slowly blinked open his eyes and smiled. 'Hey, Daddy.'

'Merry Christmas.'

'Merry Christmas.' Olly yawned and stretched, pulling his teddy in tight for a cuddle.

'Did you wake in the night?'

'I heard Santa downstairs.'

'You did?'

'I told Nell.'

'Did you? Where is she? Did she go downstairs?'

'I don't know. She took her clothes.'

Seth sat up and peered at the chair upon which Nell's clothes had rested. They were gone, and the first stirrings of alarm began to spread throughout his body. He told himself to calm down. She was probably downstairs already, having breakfast with Granny.

He looked at his watch. Just gone eight. 'We should get ready for breakfast.'

'And then can we open presents?'

He smiled. 'Of course. Come on.'

He chivvied Olly into getting ready, fetched his robe from his bedroom. There was no sign of Nell. She had to be downstairs, surely? Already eating breakfast. She was an early riser, like him. She was probably already on the black peppercorn and smoked salmon bagels and the Buck's Fizz?

He was keen to see her. To reassure himself that he was actually getting to spend Christmas with her, as he'd planned.

Olly seemed to take an age to brush his teeth and comb his hair and wash his face. Seth was getting quite twitchy! He kept telling himself not to be silly, that she'd be there, in the breakfast room, all smiles, ready to wish him a Merry Christmas. But as they headed downstairs the sense of dread he was feeling began to grow stronger and stronger. And then, just as they were about to enter the breakfast room, Jeffreys came to him with a note on a silver tray.

'Merry Christmas, my lord. This is from Miss Bryant.'

A cold lump settled in his belly. He took the slip of paper and turned to Olly. 'You go and get your breakfast with Granny. I'll be in in a moment.'

Olly nodded.

Seth dismissed Jeffreys and stood alone in the hall, afraid to open the note.

And then he did.

Seth,

I'm sorry. A million times I'm sorry. But I'm just not sure I can do this with you. I wanted to enjoy Christmas with you. You know I didn't want to be alone on Christmas Day, and I do think your family are lovely. You have all made me feel so welcome. You. Your gran. Olly.

I can deal with us. But it's not just us, is it? You come as a package deal, and Olly is the sweetest. It's not his fault. This is mine. My fault. I'm scared of what this all means and I need time to think about if it's what I want.

Please enjoy Christmas. And please don't hate me. I can't help but be afraid.

Love Nell x

His first impulse was to go rushing after her and bring her back. But then he read the letter a second time. A third time. A fourth.

Had Olly climbing into his bed been the straw to break the camel's back? She wasn't blaming Olly, but he couldn't help but think that this was what she meant. Lucas had used to wake her in the night. She'd told him that once. Had Olly doing the same thing upset her? But he was just a little boy. That was what little boys did.

She was right, though. He came as a package. Him and Olly. Him and Elmbridge, even. It was a lot for anyone to take on if they weren't used to it. Nell had been ready to bolt. One foot out through the door. Like Dana had always been. Maybe that was why he felt like he couldn't fully commit to her.

He took a moment to steady his breathing. It had become juddery and uneven. Shallow and weird.

He wouldn't get to spend Christmas with her.

His heart broke at the thought. He'd really wanted to show her Christmas, Elmbridge-style. He'd wanted to make today the best Christmas she'd ever experienced! He'd wanted to watch her open his presents. Pull crackers with her at the table. Clink champagne glasses. Go for a walk with her around the estate after dinner. Build a snowman. Sit with his arms around her in front of a crackling fire. Share a bath with her. A bed with her.

A lifetime with her.

The thought stopped him in his tracks.

A lifetime. With Nell.

He'd been afraid to want it. Afraid to tell her he did. Maybe that was why she'd run? Because she didn't know how committed he was to her. What he really felt. He'd kept telling her they would discuss it another time, but maybe that had been wrong? Maybe they should have discussed it as soon as she'd spoken about it?

Was he being crazy? Would she even want what he could offer her? Her letter said she needed time to think about what she wanted. Well, if that was the case, then surely she needed to know what her options were and what exactly he was offering?

There was still time to rescue the day.

He entered the breakfast room and pulled on the bell that would summon Jeffreys from the bowels of the house.

'Morning, Seth. Where's Nell? Still getting ready?' asked his grandmother.

'Kind of… We've just got to pop out briefly. We won't be long.'

'The hospital, is it? Try to make it back for dinner, Seth. It's *Christmas*.'

He smiled. 'I promise we won't be long.'

Jeffreys appeared. 'Yes, my lord?'

'Have my car brought round immediately, please.'

Jeffreys bowed. 'Of course, my lord.'

The flat seemed empty and cold.

Nell stood in the doorway that led into the lounge, noting the Christmas tree with no presents underneath. The Christmas cards that adorned her windowsill and mantelpiece, from friends and work colleagues. The big one in the centre from her mum and dad.

Had she made a terrible mistake? Should she have arranged to go and spend the festive season with her parents? If she had she might have avoided last night. She might have avoided running out on Seth and Olly and the lovely Dowager.

Were they awake yet?

Did they know she had gone?

She would never be able to face them again.

But the feelings that had rushed up out of nowhere when Olly had arrived in the night had been too strong and everything—*everything*—had come crashing down on her. Reality and realisation.

If she stayed with Seth, she would have to become a mother to Olly. If she stayed with Seth, she would have to become steeped in the history and tradition and responsibilities of Elmbridge. And he might realise that she wasn't up to the task of any of those.

How could she be?

She wasn't used to his world. She didn't move in his circles. She'd lost a son, and a husband who'd seemed incapable of loving her. Maybe she just wasn't deserving of all-consuming love? And Seth would realise that eventually. It was best that they just remained friends. If he still wanted her as a friend.

What she'd done was awful! Running out on him on Christmas morning? How would she ever face him again?

Entering the kitchen, she wiped away her tears and switched on the kettle. She needed a cup of tea. And then, maybe, just so she wasn't cooped up inside all day, feeling morose and miserable and alone, she'd go out for a walk. It was pretty out. It had snowed again overnight, casting everything in a fresh sprinkling of white. Painting the world afresh.

Maybe she should think about getting a cat. So she had something to come home to of an evening. A rescue cat. The mangiest, oldest cat they had. One that had been overlooked and unloved. She would give it happiness in its final years. Love it. Give it a home despite its sad history. That would be a good thing to do, right?

The kettle had long since finished boiling, but she was still standing in the kitchen, poised by the open cupboard where she kept the mugs, when there was a knock at her door.

Nell jumped in surprise, heart thundering, pulse racing.

There was only one person it could be.

Should she just pretend she wasn't at home? She could ignore the knocking and when she saw him at work in a couple of days say that she'd gone to stay with her parents after she'd left him.

But guilt, or something else, drew her to the

door. She peered through the small spyhole and saw Seth standing on the other side.

He was so close! She laid her hands against the door and then gently put her head against it, desperate to be back in his arms, but afraid to be.

Another knock. 'Nell? Are you in there?'

Yes. Yes, I'm here! And I love you so much! But I'm afraid to love you. I'm so scared.

'Nell?'

She sucked in a breath and stepped back. If he kept yelling he'd wake her neighbours, and she didn't want a scene. Maybe it was best to open the door. Explain quietly. Apologise.

The need to look into his eyes just one last time was overpowering.

Her hands reached for the lock. Turned the key.

No going back now.

She pulled open the door.

Seth looked at her.

He didn't look angry. He looked bewildered, if anything.

'Hey...'

'Hey. Can I come in?'

She dithered. Maybe it would be easier to turn his love away on the doorstep? Maybe it would be easier to be a disappointment to him while she was standing right here? But no.

She stepped back. 'Come in.'

He moved past her. That familiar scent of him filled her nose and overrode her senses, making her want to reach out and touch him.

He waited for her in the lounge. Stood staring at her as she entered.

'Talk to me,' he said.

She didn't know what to say. Or how to start. How could she explain her scary, illogical reaction of fear?

'I don't know what to say.'

'Well, let me talk, then.'

'Okay...'

She settled down on the couch next to him, ready for his onslaught of anger and disappointment.

'I'm a lot. I get that. I have a history. A title. A manor house. A grandmother. A dead girlfriend and a motherless son who is the sweetest boy I know, despite all that he has gone through. And I also have a deep and abiding love for a woman. For *you*. You're right. I come as a package deal. And that's not easy. Accepting me means accepting everything about me—and that's a lot. I know it's a huge ask, after all that you've been through. But I love you, and I believe you to be the strongest woman I know. And if anyone can handle me—us—it's you. What we have has happened fast, but the rest of it doesn't have to. We can go at your pace, move on when you're ready.'

He paused to reach out and take her hand in his.

'I'm in no rush to get you down the aisle, although one day that would be nice.' He smiled. 'And Olly's in no rush to have a new mother. You need to get to know one another. Get used to one another. I get that. And if you feel you can't do it right now, then I'll give you time. I'll give you space until you do feel ready. But please don't walk away from us because you're scared.'

He lifted her hand to his lips and kissed her fingers.

'Let me hold your hand and be by your side. Let me help you face these challenges. I believe we can have a future together. A wonderful future. A wonderful *life*.'

She looked at him, stunned that he could be so willing to wait for her!

'Oh, Seth…'

'I love you, Nell Bryant, and I would do anything to make you happy. If you need me to walk away right now, then I will. But know this. I will keep coming back for you. I will never leave you. I will be here whenever you are ready. Because you are special, and you mean so much to me. I can't adequately explain it. There aren't enough words for how you make me feel.'

He was saying all the right things! Could she do this? Would she be able to? If they went at a pace that suited her?

'But I ran out on you. What's your gran going to say?'

'She thinks you've had to go to the hospital with me for an emergency.'

Nell blinked. Okay... So Seth's gran didn't know. Nor did Olly. She didn't want the little boy to think that she had walked out on them. She knew Seth would have protected him from that, but this...this was a second chance.

Was she brave enough to take it?

'I don't know what to say...'

'Do you love me?'

She looked deeply into his eyes. Met them with an intensity of love that was impossible for her not to feel right at that moment.

'I do. With all my heart.'

'Then let's step off into the scary unknown together. Let's take a chance on this love we've found. This love that neither of us expected. Even if it is terrifying. Let's take a chance, Nell. Take it one day at a time.'

She wanted to. So much!

Tears of happiness pricked her eyes. Because he loved her, and he was willing to help her get through her days of adjusting to a new life. A life with him. She knew he would be patient and kind. She'd seen it. Experienced it. And a life without love would be empty and unfulfilling.

This was her chance.

'All right. Let's do this!' She laughed.

He beamed a smile and let out a huge breath. He must have been holding it. Then he pulled her to her feet and kissed her. Kissed her so softly and so delicately, awakening her body to want and need.

It had only been a few hours since she'd lain in his arms, but she had missed him so much!

'I love you, Seth James,' she whispered, looking directly into his eyes.

'And I love you. Are you ready to come home?'

She nodded.

She was.

Ready to go home with him.

EPILOGUE

Two years later

CHRISTMAS MORNING AND Nell awoke in her husband's arms, feeling tired and happy. Seth was draped over her, cradling her large belly, which was filled with their overdue daughter.

She could feel the baby kick and then stretch, and she had to rub at her side with her hand, to move a foot that seemed to be stuck under her ribs. It was still dark outside. Just gone five a.m. And yet she felt wide awake—as if she was waiting for something important to happen. She could sense it. An impending sense of change and expectation.

Feeling a little bit of heartburn, she managed to pull herself into a sitting position on the edge of the bed. On the bedside table was a large glass of water, so she drank a little bit—and then realised she needed the loo.

Behind her, Seth slept on, and on the far side of the bed was Olly, slumbering also.

She smiled at them both. They looked so cute lying there like that. Innocent and dreaming.

Let them sleep. We've got a long day ahead.

They had guests to take care of this year.

The first Christmas they'd spent together almost hadn't happened, because of her freaking out. The second year they'd spent it in the Alps, at a skiing resort. This year they'd decided on a proper family Christmas at home. She'd even got her mum and dad to come and stay at the manor. Mum had said she'd made her dad promise to behave.

And even though the majority of the work would be done by Jeffreys and his team, and the cook, Mrs Brough, there were still things that Nell wanted to do to make this Christmas special.

She grabbed her robe from the end of the bed and put it on, tying the belt over her large belly and waddling to the en-suite bathroom, switching on the light and closing the door gently so as not to wake her two darling boys.

Peering at herself in the mirror, she wrinkled her nose and ran a hand through her messy hair. She was just about to go to the toilet when she felt something strange.

Nell paused, glanced at her reflection again. It had been an odd sensation. As if something had…

Drip…drip…drip…

Wetness splashed onto her feet and she looked down at her toes almost in disbelief. Had her waters broken?

As if in response to her question, she felt her first contraction. Mild, low…but enough to be noticeable and to say *I'm here. Let's do this.*

Nell almost laughed in surprise and shock. Then she turned away from the loo and headed back into the darkness of the bedroom, waddling her way across the expanse of the floor to the bed. She leaned over Seth and laid a hand on his shoulder, gave him a gentle shake.

'Hey…'

Seth groaned, then blinked open his eyes suddenly. 'What's up? Is everything okay?'

'My waters have broken.'

His eyes widened and he shuffled into a sitting position. 'You're sure?'

'I've had a contraction.'

'It's baby time?'

She smiled and rubbed at her belly. 'I think so. Elise is on her way.'

He reached for her hand, squeezed it. 'You sure know how to make Christmas mornings exciting.'

She smiled. 'I know. Do you think we're ready for this?'

He cradled her face. 'I am. Are you?'

'With you by my side? I'm ready for anything.'

Seth kissed her. Then opened her robe and cradled her belly, kissing it.

What a perfect day to have another baby.

The best Christmas gift of all.

* * * * *

*If you enjoyed this story, check
out these other great reads from
Louisa Heaton*

The Brooding Doc and the Single Mom
Second Chance for the Village Nurse
Miracle Twins for the Midwife
A Date with Her Best Friend

All available now!